THE DESPERADOES
AND OTHER STORIES

This collection of stories is set in and about the West Riding town which formed the locale of Stan Barstow's first novel, *A Kind of Loving*, which was most successful.

Though there is nothing provincial in the themes of these tales, the author shows in them his continuing preoccupation with people rooted very firmly in a recognisable society. The moods vary from grave to gay, from sad to wryly humorous and reveal that Stan Barstow, while keenly aware of the tragedy of life, is also fully responsive to the humorous aspect of the human predicament.

THE DESPERADOES

AND OTHER STORIES

STAN BARSTOW

CEDRIC CHIVERS LTD
PORTWAY
BATH

First published 1961
by
Michael Joseph Ltd
This edition published
by
Cedric Chivers Ltd
by arrangement with the copyright holder
at the request of
The London & Home Counties Branch
of
The Library Association
1973

SBN 85594 911 2

Printed in Great Britain by
Redwood Press Limited, Trowbridge, Wiltshire
Bound by Cedric Chivers Ltd, Bath

For C.M.B.

Some of these stories have been broadcast by the B.B.C.
The Search for Tommy Flynn first appeared in Pick 8 of *Pick of Today's Short Stories*, published by Putnam.

CONTENTS

THE HUMAN ELEMENT

HARRY WEST's the name, fitter by trade. I'm working for Dawson Whittaker & Sons, one of the biggest engineering firms round Cressley, and lodging with Mrs Baynes, one of the firm's recommended landladies, up on Mafeking Terrace, not far from the Works. It's an interesting job – I like doing things with my hands – and not a bad screw either, what with bonus and a bit of overtime now and again, and taken all round I'm pretty satisfied. The only thing I could grumble about is some of my mates; but they're not a bad lot really. It must be because I'm a big fair bloke and the sort that likes to think a bit before he opens his mouth that gives them the idea I'm good for a laugh now and then. Some of them seem to think it's proper hilarious that I'm happy with my own company and don't need to go out boozing and skirt-chasing every night in the week to enjoy life. And on Monday mornings, sometimes, when they're feeling a bit flat after a weekend on the beer, they'll try to pull my leg about Ma Baynes and that daughter of hers, Thelma. But they get no change out of me. I just let them talk. Keep yourself to yourself and stay happy – that's my motto. I'm not interested in women anyway; I've got better ways of spending my time, not to mention my money.

I've got something better than any girl: nearly human she is. Only she wears chromium plate and black enamel instead of lipstick and nylons. And she's dependable. Look after her properly and she'll never let you down, which I reckon is more than you can say for most women. Every Saturday afternoon I tune her and polish her for the week. There's no better way of spending a Saturday afternoon: just me and the bike, and no complications. All I ask is to be left alone to enjoy it.

Well, it's summer, and a blazing hot Saturday afternoon, and I'm down on my knees in Ma Baynes's backyard with the motor bike on its stand by the wall, when a shadow falls across me and I look up and see Thelma standing there.

'Hello, Arry,' she says, and stands there looking at me with them dull, sort of khaki-coloured eyes of hers that never seem to have any expression in them, so you can't tell what she's thinking, or even if she's not thinking at all, which I reckon is usually the case.

'Oh, hello.' And I turn back to the job and give one of the spindle nuts on the front wheel a twist with the spanner.

'Are you busy?' she says then.

I'm trying my best to look that way, hoping she'll take the hint and leave me alone. 'You're allus busy with a motor bike if you look after it properly,' I say. But even me giving it to her short and off-hand like that doesn't make her shove off. Instead she flops down behind me, coming right up close so's she can get her knees on my bit of mat and pressing up against me till I can feel her big bust like a big soft cushion against my shoulder.

'What're you doing now, then?' she says.

'Well,' I say, getting ready to answer a lot of daft questions, 'I'm just checkin' 'at me front wheel's on properly. I don't want that to come loose when I'm on the move, y'know.'

'You must be clever to know all about motor bikes,' she

says, and I wonder for a second if she's sucking up to me.
But I reckon she's too simple for that.

'Oh, I don't know. You get the hang of 'em when you've
had one a bit.'

She gives a bit of a wriggle against my shoulder, sort
of massaging me with her bust. She doesn't know what
she's doing. She's like a big soft lad the way she chucks
herself about. It'd be enough to give ideas to some blokes
I could mention. But not me. It does nothing to me,
except make me feel uncomfortable. I'm breaking a
new pair of shoes in and I've cramp like needles in my
left foot. But I can't move an inch with Thelma there
behind me, else we'll both fall over.

She gives another wriggle and then gets up, nearly
knocking me into the bike headfirst. And when I've got
my balance again I stretch my leg out and move my toes
about inside the shoe.

'We was wonderin',' Thelma says, 'if you'd like to lend
us your portable radio set. Me mam wants to go on a
picnic, but me dad wants to listen to the Test Match.'

Now here's a thing. I've got to go canny here. 'Well,
er, I dunno . . .' I get up, steady, wiping my neck with
my handkerchief, giving myself time to think of an excuse
for saying no. I'm always careful with my belongings.

'Oh, we'd look after it,' Thelma says. 'On'y me dad's
that stubborn about his cricket, an' me mam won't go
without him.'

I know Old Man Baynes and his sport. It's the one
thing Ma Baynes can't override him on.

Thelma can see I'm not happy about the radio and
she says, 'Why don't you come with us, then you can look
after it yourself? We're goin' to Craddle Woods. It'll
be lovely up there today.'

I know it will, and I've already thought of having a ride out that way when I've finished cleaning the bike. But this doesn't suit me at all. I haven't been with the Bayneses long and I've been careful not to get too thick with them. Getting mixed up with people always leads to trouble sooner or later. I always reckon the world would be a sight better place if more folk kept themselves to themselves and minded their own business.

But I see that Thelma has a look on her face like a kid that wants to go to the zoo.

'Well, I'd summat else in mind really,' I say, still trying my best to fob her off. 'I was goin' to clean me bike.'

'Clean it!' she says. 'But it's clean. Look how it shines!'

'It on'y looks clean,' I say. 'There's dozens o' mucky places 'at you can't see.'

'Well, it can wait, can't it? You don't want to waste this lovely weather, do you?'

I haven't thought of wasting it, not with that nice little ride all planned. But I'm cornered. That's how it is with people. They pin you down till you can't get out any way. I can see Ma Baynes taking offence if I don't lend them the radio now, and that's the last thing I want. No trouble. I'm all for a quiet life. So I give in.

'Okay, then, I'll come. When're you settin' off?'

Thelma's face lights up like a Christmas tree at this. 'About three, I sh'd think,' she says. 'I'll tell 'em to be . . .' And then she gets her eyes fixed on something behind me and forgets what she's saying.

'Look, there's Lottie Sharpe.'

I turn round and look over into the next yard, where a girl's walking by: a slim little bit, all dressed up in nylons and high heels and even a fancy little hat.

'I wish I looked like that,' Thelma says, sort of quiet and wistful like, and I can tell she's talking to herself, not to me. I take a good look at her, standing nearly as big as me, with that sort of suet-pudding face of hers, and I see what she means, but I say nothing.

'Lottie's gettin' married next month.'

There it is: they're all alike. Getting married and spending some poor feller's brass is all they think about. I say nothing.

Thelma watches right till Lottie turns the corner into the entry, then she gives a big sigh, right down inside herself.

'I'll tell 'em to be gettin' ready, then.'

She goes back across the yard. Her overall's tight and stretched across her fat behind and I can see the red backs of her knees.

I reckon I've had it for today and I begin to pick my gear up.

We go along the street to the bus stop. Ma Baynes is walking in front, wearing white holiday shoes and carrying the sandwiches in a tartan shopping bag. Old Man Baynes, in a new cap and cricket shirt, strolls along beside her sucking at his pipe and saying nothing.

I'm walking behind with Thelma, carrying the portable radio. Thelma's changed into a thin cotton frock that's as short and tight as the overall she had on earlier. I wonder if she has any clothes she doesn't look as though she's grown out of. Now and then I take a look down at my new shoes. They're a light tan, with long toes. I've had my eye on them for weeks, along with a pair with inch-thick crêpe soles, and I've had a lot of trouble making up my mind between them. But these are

definitely dressier: a smashing pair of shoes. They'll
be fine when a bit of the newness has worn off. Just now
they've developed a bit of a squeak and once Thelma
looks down and giggles. I give her a look and move away
from her and try to look as if I'm not with them at all,
and hoping like mad we won't run into any of the bods
from the Works.

We sit downstairs on the bus. Just out of manners I
have a bit of a difference with Old Man Baynes about
who's going to get the fares. But I soon give in when I
see one or two of the other passengers looking round. It's
the Bayneses' treat anyway and I don't want to attract
attention and have everybody taking me for Thelma's
young man. She's sitting next to me, by the window.
She's chattering all the time to her mother in front and
bouncing backwards and forwards like a kid on a trip.
Her skirt's getting well up past her knees and I can feel
her leg hot when it rubs mine, so I move over to the edge
of the seat and look at the barber's rash on the back of
Old Man Baynes's neck.

In about twenty minutes we're well out in the country
and we get off the bus and cross the road and take a
path through a field of corn that's ready for getting in,
it's so heavy and ripe, and as still as if we were seeing it
on a photo. It's a real scorcher of a day. We go round the
edge of the farmyard and down into the woods. The
trees come over and shut the sun out and the path's
narrow and steep. We walk in single file with Ma Baynes
in front and every now and then one of us trips over the
roots that stick out of the ground all hard and shiny
like the veins on the backs of old people's hands. After a
bit of this we come out into a clearing. Down the hill
we can see the beck with the sun shining on it and on the

far side there's a golf course with one or two nobs having a game. Past that there's fields stretching miles off and electricity pylons marching along like something out of a science-fiction picture.

'This'll do,' Ma Baynes says and drops her bag and flops down on the grass like half a ton of sand. Old Man Baynes shoots me a look and I pass the radio over. He takes it out of the case and switches on, stretching out on the grass with his ear stuck right up to the speaker as though he thinks the set's too little to make much noise.

Ma Baynes levers her shoes off and pushes the hair off her forehead. Then she clasps her hands in her lap and gives a satisfied look all round.

'We sh'd come here more often,' she says, ' 'stead o' stickin' in that mucky old town.' She gives Thelma and me a funny look. 'Me an' your father used to come courtin' here,' she says. 'Didn't we, George?'

Old Man Baynes just says 'Mmmm?' and Ma Baynes twists her head and pins him with a real sharp look.

'I hope you're not goin' to have your head stuck inside that thing all afternoon,' she says. 'If that's all you can find to do you might as well ha' stopped at home.'

'That's what I wanted to do,' he says, and gives the radio a tap with his finger. 'I can't get no reception.' He picks the set up and gives it a shake.

'Here,' I say, 'let me.'

Ma Baynes gives a sigh. 'Here we are, next to nature, an' all they can find to do is fiddle wi' a wireless set!'

After a bit she sends Thelma up to the farm for a jug of tea. By this time me and Old Man Baynes between us have taken so many parts out of the radio it'd take a chopper to strip it down any more. All the guts of it are spread out in one of my hankies on the grass and I'm looking at them in a bit of a daze, wondering if we haven't gone a bit too far.

Old Man Baynes has lost all interest. He's sitting by himself, looking out over the valley, chewing grass stalks and muttering to himself something like, 'I wonder how they're gettin' on . . .' He's worried sick about that cricket match.

Soon Thelma comes back with the tea and Ma Baynes sets the mugs out. 'Come on, you men, and get your teas.'

We get going on the fishpaste sandwiches. Nobody has much to say now. It's all right going out into the country, but what do you do when you get there? It begins to get me down after a bit and I get to thinking about the bike and all I could be doing with her if I wasn't wasting my time sitting here.

When we've finished Thelma picks up the jug.

'I'll take that back, if you like,' I say. I think a walk might help to pass the time.

Ma Baynes looks up at us. 'Why don't you both go?'

I'd rather go on my own, but I give a shrug. 'If you like.'

We set off up the path under the trees. It's a bit cooler here but I'm still sweating a lot and my shirt's stuck to me. Thelma's the same. Her frock was tight to start with and now it looks as if it's been pasted on her. We get the full force of the sun as we leave the shade on the edge of the farmyard, and it's dazzling the way it bounces back off the whitewashed walls. Everything's dead quiet and there's no sign of life except for a few hens pecking around and a great red rooster strutting about among them as though he owns the place. I put my hand down on the flagstones as Thelma comes back from the house.

'Could fry your breakfast on here,' I say, just to help the conversation on a bit.

'It is hot, in't it?' she says, and flaps her arms about like an angry old hen. 'I wish we was at the seaside; I'd love to be in the sea just now.'

We go back into the wood and follow the path till we come to another one, narrower and steeper, leading off down through the bracken to the beck.

'Let's go down here,' Thelma says, and starts off before I can say yea or nay. She runs on in front and I follow, and when I come out on the grassy bank where the stream bends she's sitting down taking her sandals off.

'I'm goinna paddle,' she says. 'Comin'?'

Paddling's nothing in my line so I shake my head and stretch out on the bank while she goes in. I chew a grass stalk and watch her bounce about in the water like a young hippo, holding her skirt up and giving me a good view of her legs above the knee.

Before long she's overdoing the jumping about a bit and I tell her to be careful of the stones on the bottom; but she just laughs and jumps right up out of the water. Well, it's her funeral, I'm just thinking, when her face changes and she starts to sway about and throw her arms out to keep her balance. I don't take this in for a second, and then I see she's not acting any more, and I jump up. The next thing I know my right leg's in water up to the knee and my arm's round her holding her up. I shift my hand to get a better hold and feel my fingers sink into her soft bust.

When I have her safe on the bank I take a look at my

sopping trouser leg and shoe. But I'm not bothering about them somehow. It's my hand. Something's wrong with it. It's still got the feel of Thelma's bust in the fingers.

I look at her sprawling on the grass with her knees up. 'You've grazed your foot.' She's a bit short of wind and doesn't say anything, so I kneel down in front of her and dry her foot on my spare hankie and then tie the hankie round it in a makeshift bandage. 'That'll stop your shoe rubbing it till you get home.'

When I lift my eyes I find I'm looking straight along her leg to her pink pants and what with this and that funny feeling in my hand I look away quick and feel myself coming up brick red.

She puts her leg down and leans forward to feel at the bandage. I stand up out of the way.

'I don't know what I'd've done if you hadn't been here, Arry,' she says.

'You'd ha' got wet,' I say, and give a short laugh. And all the time I'm looking down at her big bust lolling about inside her frock. She's got nothing much else on besides the frock and it looks as though if she leans over a bit further the whole flipping lot might come flopping out, and I can't keep my eyes off it, wondering what I'll do if it does. I don't know what's come over me.

Then all at once a funny thing happens. As sharp as if it was yesterday I remember the time we went with the school to the Art Gallery. It's the only time I've ever been but I remember clear as daylight all them naked women, big strapping women, lolling about on red plush, as brazen as you please. And it comes to me that Thelma would have been just right in them days: they must all have been like Thelma then. I shut my eyes and imagine her and then I begin to get excited. It's like a great bubble filling all inside me and then it goes down and leaves me all loose and wobbly where my guts should be. God! but I've never felt like this before. I put my hand out and I can't keep it steady.

'It's ever so nice havin' some'dy big an' strong to look after you,' Thelma's saying.

'I like looking after you,' I say. My throat's all clogged up and I swallow hard to clear it. 'I . . . I'd like to look after you all along.'

Thelma stares and goes as red as fire. 'Would you, Arry? All along?'

I give her a nod because I can't talk any more, and sit down beside her. The way I'm feeling now I'd tell her anything.

'I allus knew you was a nice lad, Arry,' she says, and hides her face as I slide my arm round her waist and try to pull her over.

'Give us a kiss, then,' I say.

She doesn't move for a couple of seconds, then she turns her face round and turns it straight back again just as I'm making for her and I end up kissing her on the ear. We sit like that for a minute or two and then I try to touch her bust again. She gives a wriggle at this.

'We'd best be gettin' back, Arry,' she says. 'They'll be wonderin' where we've got to.'

She pulls her sandals on and we stand up. I grab her and plonk her one straight on the mouth. Her eyes flutter like bees' wings after that.

'You'll have to let me lean on you, Arry,' she says, all soft and melting like.

We get back to the main path and make for the clearing. Thelma limps along the path and I charge along through the bracken with my arm round her waist. As we get near the place where we left Ma and Old Man Baynes I begin to notice she's leaning on me fit for a broken leg, let alone a scratched foot. And I can feel my trouser leg all sopping wet and my foot squelching away in my shoe. The next minute I see Ma and Old Man Baynes sitting there waiting for us and all the feeling I had by the beck's gone and I just feel like turning round and running for it.

Thelma tells her everything and a bit more besides, nearly falling over herself to get it all out.

'An' guess what, Mam!' she says at the end. 'Me an' Arry's engaged!'

Even Old Man Baynes lifts his eyebrows at this and I feel myself go all cold at the glitter that comes into Ma Baynes's eyes.

When we get home Thelma offers to press my trousers. I reckon it's the least she can do, so I go upstairs and change and bring them down to her. She spreads them out on the kitchen table and sets about them with her mother's electric iron.

'That's right, love,' Ma Baynes says. 'Get your hand in.'

She's settled down with a box of chocolates and a woman's paper, and there's a variety show on the wireless. Old Man Baynes chucks his sports final down and takes his glasses off. 'Would you believe it?' he says. 'Rain stopped play. An' we haven't had a drop all day!'

I make some excuse and go up to my room where I can be on my own and think a bit and try to sort it all out. I sit down on the bed and look at my shoes standing under a chair. I've already polished them with a rag and one's bright and shiny, but the other one's soggy and dull. I can't see that one ever polishing up again. I really can't. Anyway, they'll never do for best again. New on at that. I think now that I could have reckoned the radio was bust when Thelma first asked me. I don't think fast enough by half, that's my trouble. It's bust now, though, right enough. A fiver that'll cost me, if a penny. The shoes and the radio. And on top of all that I've gone and got myself engaged! Fifteen quid for a ring, and Ma Baynes for a mother-in-law. How I ever came to do it I'll never know. But I'll have to get out of it somehow, even if it means finding fresh digs; which is a pity because I've just nicely got settled here. I'll have to think about it. But not now. I can't concentrate now. I'll think about it later when I haven't got so much else on my mind. Just now I can't get over the shoes. I've had plenty of enjoyment out of the radio, but I've only worn the shoes today. A new pair of shoes like that; ruined first time on. A smashing pair of shoes, and they're done. It doesn't bear thinking about.

I sit there on the bed and I hear laughing coming up from the wireless in the kitchen. It sounds as though they're laughing at me. I begin to think what a nice life these hermit bods must have with nobody to bother them; and then I seem to go off into a sort of doze, because when I come to again it's dark and I can't see the shoes any more.

FREESTONE AT THE FAIR

IT was only afterwards that it occurred to Freestone to wonder why the gipsy should have picked on him rather than Emily or Charlie, and the thought that he might have looked the most gullible of the three never entered his mind. For when, after pondering the matter for a moment or two, he seemed to recall the woman's saying he had an interesting face, he was instantly satisfied with that eminently reasonable explanation. For there were deeper aspects of the matter concerning him by this time: aspects which might have had grave effects on the mind and reason of a lesser man.

She had stood in the opening of her tent and fixed on him a dark and lustrous eye. Her sultry stare did not perturb him and his natural inclination, when she offered to read his hand, was to walk on, ignoring the rapid mumbled persuasions. But to his surprise he found himself being pressed into acceptance by his companions.

His surprise contained more than a little irritation, for this was the third time that day they had formed an alliance against him. (But for them he would never have thought of visiting the fair in the first place, and only a few minutes ago they had failed to entice him to join them while they sampled the undignified thrills and delights of the Whip.)

Mrs Freestone, her yellow-brown eyes and plump face shining with the unaccustomed excitement, urged him on.

'Go on, Percy,' she said. 'See what she tells you.'

Since Emily was aware of his views on fortune-telling, as she was on most other subjects, Freestone considered this to be nothing less than wanton betrayal and his mind began instinctively to frame a future reprimand.

Charlie, fifteen stone of jovial, arrogant manhood, was, of course, all for it.

'Ye-es, go on and have a bash, Perce,' he said, giving Freestone a playful thump on the upper arm.

Freestone frowned at the unwelcome familiarity of the blow and the detestable abbreviation of his Christian name. He had for some time past regretted the generous impulse which had prompted him to offer Charlie accommodation while he looked for suitable rooms. He regarded it now as a lapse, a temporary mental aberration; whereas it had seemed such a naturally kindly thing to do at the time the Manager had introduced them and intimated that Charlie was the son of an old friend of his and was learning the business in preparation for higher things. Now the few days originally specified had stretched into several weeks and Freestone was finding Charlie's all-good-pals-together attitude to life simply too much at such close range. And the fact that he himself was manager of Soft Furnishings while Charlie, his supposed influence apparently not at all what it had at first seemed to be, was still a mere assistant in Hardware, loaded an already painful situation with an additional sting.

'Well really,' Freestone said now, with the intention of killing the matter with a few scornful words. 'There's absolutely no foundation to this fortune-telling business, you know. It's simply a catchpenny from first to last.'

But he seemed temporarily to have lost Emily, and Charlie was impervious to scorn in any shape or form.

'Oh, come off it, Perce!' he said with dreadful joviality. 'Let yourself go, man! Show a bit of holiday spirit! You'll get a laugh out of it if nothing else.'

And on to the camel's back of Freestone's resistance Charlie then blithely tossed the last straw.

'You're not scared of what she might tell you, are you?'

Thus challenged, Freestone had no choice.

'Very well, then,' he said, with the lofty resignation of one who spends a large part of his life humouring the whims of the sub-intelligent. 'But it's nothing but foolishness to encourage these charlatans.'

With an instinctive gesture he lifted his hand to adjust the rim of his bowler hat, only to encounter instead the unfamiliar peak of the tweed cap which he had always hitherto considered a sufficient concession to the 'holiday spirit.' It was a psychological setback from which he recovered admirably, and with one hand resting lightly in the breast of his dark blue blazer—rather in the manner of a certain deceased foreign dignitary of similar stature, but immeasurably greater significance—he marched with a firm and dignified tread into the dark interior of the tent.

There was a lot of what looked like black-out material draped about to add to the atmosphere of mystery, but a modern adjustable reading-lamp with a weak down-shaded bulb occupied the place of the traditional crystal ball on the table in the middle of the tent. A voice from the shadows bade Freestone sit down and he obeyed, perching gingerly on the edge of a collapsible chair which sloped alarmingly in its stance on the uneven turf. A rather grubby hand appeared under the light. Freestone primed it with a two-shilling piece and replaced it with his own pink and well scrubbed palm.

The woman began by tracing Freestone's character, revealing all those sterling qualities, the possession of which he had never had occasion to doubt.

'I am looking into the future now,' the gipsy said at length. 'It is very hard. You are not responsive. You doubt my powers.'

Sighing at the waste of money, Freestone passed over another florin.

'You are a family man,' the woman said.

'Oh, but I'm not,' Freestone said.

'You will be, very soon. I see a child. A boy, I think. And a time of rejoicing. You have waited a long time.'

'And what after that?' Freestone said, smirking disbelievingly. 'Why not make it twins?'

'You are not sympathetic,' the woman said. 'You do not believe. It is not safe to scoff at those who have the power to pierce the dark mystery of the future.'

'*Make* me believe,' Freestone challenged her. 'Tell me more.'

'I see,' the woman said. 'I see—' and with a gasp she thrust Freestone's hand from her.

He was immediately interested. 'What?' he said. 'What do you see?'

'It is nothing. I cannot tell.'

Recklessly, Freestone took a ten-shilling note from his wallet and laid it on the table. He extended his hand over it.

'Tell me what you see.'

The brown forefinger crawled over his palm and despite himself Freestone felt his spine chill as the woman said:

'Death. I see death.'

She set up a queer soft moaning under her breath and Freestone's flesh crawled.

'Is it the child's death you see?'

'No, not the child. The child is well, three months old. It is the father I can see—'

Freestone snatched his hand away. 'Are you trying to frighten me?' he said harshly. The woman grabbed the ten-shilling note from the table.

'You are unsympathetic.'

'You trek about the countryside,' Freestone said. 'Never do an honest day's work from one year to the next; preying on gullible people . . . Well let me tell you you've picked on the wrong man this time. I've half a mind to report you to the police.'

'I have said nothing,' the woman said. 'Please go.'

Freestone went out, bristling. He admitted to himself that she had given him quite a turn; but he was all right again when he had been out in the light and the fresh air for a few minutes; and he took pleasure in exacting a small revenge on Emily and Charlie by refusing to disclose anything but the few generalities from the beginning of the session.

Charlie felt for his loose silver. 'Here, let me have a go.' He disappeared into the tent and the Freestones stood and waited in silence. Ten minutes passed before he came out again.

'Well?' said Emily eagerly.

'Oh, the usual things,' Charlie said dismissing it with a shrug. 'I'm to watch out for a tall dark man on a sea voyage.' He laughed. 'Come on, let's go knock coconuts down.'

'Pure poppycock,' Freestone said, enjoying the disappointment on Emily's face. He was thinking that there was at least one serious flaw in the gipsy's prophecy. Emily was a barren wife, which was the sole reason for their present childless state. It had rankled with him for years, and thinking of the gipsy's words renewed the irritation. He looked about him as they strolled along at the parents and children thronging the fairground and reflected bitterly on the unkind Providence which had given him such a colourless and useless mate. He stared irritably at the lock of mouse-brown hair which had come untidily astray from Emily's bun, and when she spoke to him he snapped her into a miserable silence.

In his constant pre-occupation with the smooth functioning of Soft Furnishings the incident became dismissed from Freestone's mind and he thought no more of it until some seven or eight months later.

He had just passed through a trying period culminating in the departure for fresh pastures of Charlie Lofthouse, when it had been made clear even to his thick-skinned self that his stay could not be indefinitely prolonged. No sooner, it seemed, had the Freestones resumed their placid and dignified pre-Charlie mode of living that Emily blushingly informed her husband that she was with child. Freestone was amazed and delighted, and it was not until the initial excitement had faded slightly that he remembered the incident at the fair. Resolutely he pushed it back into oblivion and managed to keep it there until after the birth of the child.

It was a boy, and the Freestones lavished on it all the obsessive affection of the middle-aged for their first-born. Congratulations were showered on them from all sides, not least from the staff of Soft Furnishings, who hoped with the coming of this new interest into his life for a mellowing of Freestone's personality and a relaxation of his iron rule.

It became obvious by the time the child was two months

old that so far as physical resemblances were concerned Freestone ran a poor second to Emily. And there were those who, not knowing him well, were tactless enough to point this out. But Freestone dismissed physical likenesses as being of little importance and did not hesitate to assure the people concerned of his faith in the child's revealing, all in good time, its inheritance of his own intellect and general strength of character.

And then one day Freestone awoke from his intoxicated state and remembered the child's age. Now, despite all his scepticism, he could not entirely erase the gipsy's words from his mind, and on the night the boy was three months old he slept badly, imagining strange pains in his chest and disturbed by unusual dreams. But he was at the store as usual the next morning and at five minutes to nine, after tidying himself up in the cloakroom, he took his usual stance in the middle of his domain in preparation for the first of the day's customers.

It was at half-past ten that the Manager summoned Freestone to his office, thinking that as he had known him best he should be the first to hear of the sad and sudden end of Charlie Lofthouse.

As the full significance of what his superior was saying smote Freestone he blanched visibly and put his hand on the desk as though for support.

'Did you know he had heart disease?' the Manager asked.

Freestone shook his head. 'He was such an athletic-looking chap,' he said weakly.

The Manager tut-tutted and pursed his lips. 'You never can tell,' he said profoundly. He looked up into Freestone's pasty face. 'It must have come as a bit of a shock to you,' he said. 'Perhaps you'd better go and sit down for a while.'

Freestone took the Manager at his word and for the next twenty minutes Soft Furnishings rubbed along without his guiding hand, while he sat locked in one of the cubicles in the cloakroom, alone with his thoughts. Nor did he show any of his usual sparkle and grip for the rest of the morning. His staff were quick to notice this and, though he was far from popular, sympathise once the news had got about.

At lunch, Freestone sat opposite Cartwright, who managed Men's Tailoring. Inevitably the conversation turned to the sudden end of Charlie, with added observations on the odd tricks of life in general.

Now Cartwright was a hard-headed, worldly type, Freestone thought.

'What do you know about fortune-telling?' he asked over coffee.

'You mean the crystal ball, playing cards, and all that?'

'Yes, reading the future in general. In a person's hand, for instance. I was reading something last night which set me wondering. Do you think a fortune-teller could read what would happen to one person in the hand of another?'

Cartwright stirred his coffee and thought about Freestone's question. 'If the prophecy were to have an effect on the life of the person whose hand was being read, I suppose it's feasible.' He tasted his coffee, added enough sugar to cover a sixpence, and tasted it again. 'Always allowing you believe in the business in the first place, that is,' he said. 'And ninety per cent of it's pure charlatanism, of course.'

'My own opinion exactly,' Freestone said. There was nothing like talking to somebody sensible for getting things into perspective.

'Though there are more things in heaven and earth . . .'
Cartwright said. 'For instance, I have a cousin who once
received a communication from a dead friend.'

'Spiritualism?' Freestone said disbelievingly.

'That's one name for it. Very interesting, you know,
when you come to look into it . . .'

Freestone stood up. 'I'm sorry. I've just remembered
something I must attend to.'

Well, well. Cartwright of all people. Who would have
thought it? It shook him. And he remained shaken until
towards the end of the afternoon when, at last, he seemed
to come to a decision. At six o'clock, when he stepped
from the store on his way home, he had the air of a man
who has spent a long period looking deep inside himself
and has emerged satisfied with what he has seen.

Emily's behaviour reassured him further. For when he
told her of poor Charlie Lofthouse lying stiff and cold in
his lonely room, his laughter silenced for ever in this
world, she displayed what seemed to him to be no more
than an appropriate interest and concern. People were
born and people died. Life went on . . .

Especially did life go on, for as they sat by the fire
after supper a cry from upstairs brought Emily to her feet
with an exclamation of annoyance. 'Your son has been
behaving badly all day,' she said. 'I've been able to get
hardly anything done.'

They went up together and Freestone peered into the
cot. The crying ceased.

'Ah!' said Freestone, 'he knows his father is here now
and that he must be good. Yes he does, doesn't he? Yes
he does. Tchk tchk, tchk . . .'

He bent over the cot and chucked dotingly to the
child.

Later, sitting once more by the fire, Freestone paused in the act of reaching for the evening paper.

'You look to have something on your mind.'

'I was just thinking of poor Charlie Lofthouse,' Emily said.

'Oh?'

'Yes. You know, he wasn't really a bad sort of fellow.'

'No, no, not a bad sort,' Freestone said generously. 'Not *our* type, of course.'

'You remember that day we all went to the fair together,' Emily said, 'and you and he had your palms read?'

'Oh, yes, yes, I do recall it.' Freestone looked keenly at Emily.

'He mentioned afterwards that she'd told him he would have a long life, and children.' Mrs Freestone's eyes met her husband's. 'And the poor man didn't have either, did he?'

For perhaps five seconds their glances were locked. Then Freestone lifted his paper and shook it open.

'Haven't I always said that fortune-telling is poppy-cock?' he said.

THE END OF AN OLD SONG

HE was already awake on Christmas morning when she went in to draw back the curtains. He watched her from the prison of his bed and his first words were:

'D'you think t'band'll call this mornin'?'

'I should think so,' she said in an off-hand tone as she admitted the grey half-light into the room and then came bustling over to tidy the bedclothes about his wasted form. 'They said they would, didn't they?'

'Aye,' her husband said. 'Aye, they said so.'

She stood by the bed, looking down at him with fretful concern in her eyes. 'Haven't you slept?'

He stirred sluggishly under the sheets. 'Oh, on an' off,' he said listlessly. His eyes wandered. 'I wonder what time they'll come,' he said in a moment.

Anticipation of the band's visit had been the only thing in his life during the last few days, outside herself and his bed and the four too familiar walls. But she no longer resented his pre-occupation: he was helpless now and this was all that was left to him of his lifelong passion. She was in command.

He had been in his uniform when she first met him, while strolling through the park on a summer Sunday afternoon. She was nineteen then and thought how handsome and military-like he looked in his scarlet tunic and shiny-peaked cap with its gold lyre and braid. But his playing had become a constant source of friction between them during the forty years of their marriage

before the accident. What had first attracted her to him
became anathema to her and she never grew used to taking
second place to his music.

'But it in't a case o' taking second place,' he had said
to her shortly after their marriage. 'You knew I played wi'
t'band afore you wed me.'

'I thought when you were married your wife 'ud be
more important to you than your banding,' was her reply.

'But you don't want to look at it like that,' he said.
'Don't make it sound as though I don't think owt about
you!' He told her that she should go with him and mix
with the other bandsmen's wives; but she had notions of
gentility and liked to choose her company.

'I can't stand that crowd wi' their drinkin' an' carryin'
on,' she said.

He tried to persuade her that she would find grand
women among them if only she would take the trouble
to be sociable and get to know them. But she saw it as a
test of strength and refused to give in. He went his own
way and in the days and evenings without him she knew
her defeat.

And then two years ago, twelve months before he was
due to retire, a careless step on a muddy scaffolding had
given him to her. She had devoted herself to his care,
agonising for him with a feeling she had thought long
dried up and finding a bitter satisfaction in the knowledge
that he would be dependent on her for the rest of his days,
and that the hated music could never take him away
again.

Once more when she gave him his breakfast, and yet
again when she went up to wash and tidy him for the day,
the focus of his thoughts was revealed.

'Have you heard owt on 'em yet? Can you hear 'em

anywhere about?' And at her negative reply: 'I wonder if they've decided to leave it till Boxin' Day.'

The excitement showed in two dull spots of colour in his pale cheeks. It was the only sign of spirit in him and it disturbed her.

'Nah don't you go gettin' all worked up about it,' she admonished him. 'They'll come all in good time. Why, they'll hardly have gotten out of their beds by now!'

He lay back weakly among the pillows while she sponged his face and hands and chest. He had been a big man once and quietly proud of his physique; but now the flesh was gone and the skin taut across the cage of his ribs. She wondered vaguely, as she had wondered so many times before, how long it could go on. The doctors could not tell her. He might last for years, they said; or he might go at any time. She must be ready for that. The only thing they were sure of was that he would never leave his bed again.

But she had a strange feeling about him lately. She felt that something was going to happen and she had prepared herself for the worst, which, she told herself, could only be a mercy for him. He had not been himself these past few days. He had no interest in anything but the band's expected visit and he made no effort to do even the small things he had always insisted on doing for himself, but rested passively, listlessly between the sheets while she hovered about him with brisk and dedicated efficiency.

'Don't you feel well?' she asked him as she put aside the bowl of grey, soapy water and drew the blankets up round him.

'I'm all right, I reckon.'

'You don't feel any pain anywhere, do you?' she said.

'No more than usual, I mean. You wouldn't like me to ask the doctor to call?'

He moved his cropped grey head against the pillows. 'No,' he said. 'I'm just tired, that's all. I feel tired out.'

He closed his eyes and she sighed and left him, going down stairs shaking her head.

It was almost half-past eleven before she heard from her kitchen the distant strains of the band as it played its first piece in the street. She wondered if her husband could hear it too and she went to the foot of the stairs and called out to him to listen. Some twenty minutes later there was the sound of voices and the shuffle of feet in the entry, and when she peered out through the lace curtains she saw the score or so of musicians forming a circle in the yard.

They struck off with *Christians, Awake!* and followed with *Hark! the Herald Angels Sing* and *Come, All Ye Faithful*. They stopped then and during the ensueing mumble of conversation there came a knock on the door. When she opened the door the conductor, in mufti, was on the step. He leaned forward across the threshold, his breath like steam.

'Is he listenin'?' he said in a low, hoarse tone, as though he and the women shared some secret kept from the man upstairs. His eyes swivelled skywards as he spoke.

'Aye, he's listenin',' she said, wiping her hands on her apron. 'He's been on edge all mornin', wonderin' if you'd forgotten him.'

The conductor's eyes opened wide with ingenuous surprise. 'Nay, Missis, he ought to know we'd never let him down.'

'I told him as much.'

The man leaned closer and she recoiled slightly from the smell of whisky that always awaited the band on Christmas morning at the mill-owner's house up the street. His voice sank to a hoarse conspiratorial whisper. 'Will you ask him if there's owt special he'd like us to play for him?' He nudged her arm. 'Go on, Missis. Nip up an' ask him. We'll give him a Command Performance.'

She went through the kitchen and up into the bedroom. He watched her come in with eyes that were brighter than before.

'I thowt they'd come,' he said. 'I thowt they wouldn't forget me.'

'Didn't I tell you so?' she said. 'Gettin' yourself all worked up like that . . .'

'How many on 'em?' he said.

She told him, about twenty, and he nodded. She could see it pleased him.

'A good turn-out.'

'They want to know if there's owt special you'd like 'em to play for you.'

He thought for a moment, then said slowly, 'I think I'd like 'em to play *Abide with Me*. That's all, I think.'

'All right.' She turned to go. 'I'll tell 'em.'

Then as she moved through the doorway he called softly to her, 'Ey!' and she stopped and turned back into the room. His expression was quietly eager and at the same time curiously bashful as he said, 'D'you think . . .' He stopped. 'D'you think you could get me me cornet?'

She was taken off balance and surprise put an edge on her voice. 'What ever for?' she said. 'You can't play it.'

'I know,' he said. He looked away from her. 'I'd just like to have it.'

There was an expression in his pale eyes which she could not fathom, but it made her cross the room and rummage in the bottom of the built-in wardrobe till she found the instrument case. She took the cornet out of the case and put it on the bed beside him.

'Is t'mouthpiece theer an' all?'

She took the mouthpiece from its pocket and fitted it into the cornet, then watched him, suspicious and puzzled, and somehow disturbed.

'All reight,' he said then. 'That's all.'

When she had gone downstairs again he brought one arm from under the sheets and took hold of the cornet, his fingers feeling for the valves. He lay waiting and in a little while the band started the hymn in the yard below his window. He listened as the treble instruments followed the long-drawn-out and solemn melody, the soprano cornet adding its soaring sweetness to the melodic line, while below the bass instruments filled out the texture of sound with deep, rich, organ-like chords and the bass drum marked off the rhythm with its slow and ponderous beat. He thought of many things as he listened: of his days as a boy with the band; of the first world war and playing through French towns on the way to the front line. He thought of bright peacetime afternoons of concerts and on the march; and contests all over the country—Huddersfield, Leicester, Scarborough, and the finest of them all at the Crystal Palace and Belle Vue. It was as though his whole life, irrevocably bound up with music, passed through his mind as the music swelled and filled the yard and his room with a sound so noble and so moving that his eyes brimmed over and the tears rolled softly, silently down his cheeks.

Downstairs in the kitchen the woman hummed the

hymn to herself as she peeled potatoes for the Christmas dinner. She thought as she worked of her husband and how many times he had 'played out' with the band at Christmas; and guiltily she savoured the bitter sweetness of her triumph.

When the music ceased she wiped her hands and took her purse before the knock came again.

'D'you think he'd like one'r two on us to pop up an' have a word with him?' the conductor asked.

Some of the old resentment stirred in her. She looked down at the man's dirty shoes and thought of them on her stair carpet and she said:

'No, I think not. He's not been too well these last few days. Best leave it a day or two.'

The man nodded. 'Just as you like, Missis. Well, I hope he liked it. It allus war his favourite.' He stood musing for a moment as the last of the bandsmen made his slow way out of the yard and down the entry. 'I got to thinkin' when we were playin' on how many happy times we've had together, us an owd John . . .' He sighed and shook his head. 'Ah, well, it comes to us all, I reckon. We'd best be gerrin' about us rounds. Wish him a happy Christmas thru all on us. An' the same to you, Missis.'

She felt in her purse as he moved away from the door. 'Here . . .'

He turned and recoiled, shocked. 'Nay, Missis, we don't want owt thru you! We didn't come here for that. This is a special call.'

She saw that she had offended him but she persisted, pressing the shilling into the mittened hand. 'We can pay for all we get yet,' she said. 'We're not in need o' charity.'

He avoided her eyes, the sympathetic friendliness gone

from his face, leaving only a painful grimace of embarrassment.

'Just as you like, Missis,' he said.

She carried on with her work when they had gone and more than an hour passed by before she went upstairs again. There was something about the silence in the room which stopped her in the doorway. She knew at once that this was deeper than the silence of sleep and though she had thought herself prepared for it, the shock was like a blow to the heart.

She stepped into the room, her eyes falling on him as he lay there, his head deep in the pillows, the cold cornet under his hand. The moisture of his tears was gone from his cheeks and it was a new expression which stopped her short again. It was a smile, a smile of such happiness and deep contentment that it seemed to her that at that very moment he must be hearing down the rolling vaults of the Great Beyond the soaring of the cornets, the thunder of the basses, and the throbbing of the drum.

And she knew that to the very end she was defeated.

ONE OF THE VIRTUES

THE watch belonged to my grandfather and it hung on a hook by the head of his bed where he had lain for many long weeks. The face was marked off in Roman numerals, the most elegant figures I had ever seen. The case was of gold, heavy and beautifully chased; and the chain was of gold too, and wonderfully rich and smooth in the hand. The mechanism, when you held the watch to your ear, gave such a deep, steady ticking that you could not imagine its ever going wrong. It was altogether a most magnificent watch and when I sat with my grandfather in the late afternoon, after school, I could not keep my eyes away from it, dreaming that someday I too might own such a watch.

It was almost a ritual for me to sit with my grandfather for a little while after tea. My mother said he was old and drawing near his time, and it seemed to me that he must be an incredible age. He liked me to read to him from the evening paper while he lay there, his long hands, soft and white now from disuse and fined down to skin and bone by illness and age, fluttered restlessly about over the sheets, like a blind man reading braille. He had never been much of a reader himself and it was too much of an effort for him now. Possibly because he had had so little education, no one believed in it more, and he was always eager for news of my progress at school. The day I brought home the news of my success in the County Minor Scholarship examination he sent out for half an ounce of twist and found the strength to sit up in bed for a smoke.

'Grammar School next, then, Will?' he said, pleased as Punch.

'Then college,' I said, seeing the path straight before me. 'Then I shall be a doctor.'

'Aye, that he will, I've no doubt,' my grandfather said. 'But he'll need plenty o' patience afore that day. Patience an' hard work, Will lad.'

Though, as I have said, he had little book-learning, I thought sometimes as I sat with my grandfather that he must be one of the wisest men in Yorkshire; and these two qualities – patience and the ability to work hard – were the cornerstones of his philosophy of life.

'Yes, Grandad,' I told him. 'I can wait.'

'Aye, Will, that's t'way to do it. That's t'way to get on, lad.'

The smoke was irritating his throat and he laid aside the pipe with a sigh that seemed to me to contain regret for all the bygone pleasures of a lifetime and he fidgeted with the sheets. 'It must be gettin' on, Will . . .'

I took down the watch and gave it to him. He gazed at it for some moments, winding it up a few turns. When he passed it back to me I held it, feeling the weight of it.

'I reckon he'll be after a watch like that hisself, one day, eh, Will?'

I smiled shyly, for I had not meant to covet the watch so openly. 'Someday, Grandad,' I said. I could never *really* imagine the day such a watch could be mine.

'That watch wa' gi'n me for fifty year o' service wi' my firm,' my grandfather said. ' "A token of appreciation," they said . . . It's theer, in t'back, for you to see . . .'

I opened the back and looked at the inscription there: 'For loyal service . . .'

Fifty years . . . My grandfather had been a blacksmith. It was hard now to believe that these pale, almost transparent hands had held the giant tongs or directed the hammer in its mighty downward swing. Fifty years . . . Five times my own age. And the watch, prize of hard work and loyalty, hung, proudly cherished, at the head of the bed in which he was resting out his days. I think my grandfather spoke to me as he did partly because of the great difference in our ages and partly because of my father. My mother never spoke of my father and it was my grandfather who cut away some of the mystery with which my mother's silence had shrouded him. My father, Grandfather told me, had been a promising young man cursed with a weakness. Impatience was his weakness: he was impatient to make money, to be a success, to impress his friends; and he lacked the perseverance to approach success steadily. One after the other he abandoned his projects, and he and my mother were often unsure of their next meal. Then at last, while I was still learning to walk, my father, reviling the lack of opportunity in the mother country, set off for the other side of the world and was never heard of again. All this my grandfather told me, not with bitterness or anger, for I gathered he had liked my father, but with sorrow that a good man should have gone astray for want of what, to my grandfather, was a simple virtue, and brought such a hard life to my mother, Grandfather's daughter.

So my grandfather drifted to the end; and remembering those restless fingers I believe he came as near to losing his patience then as at any time in his long life.

One evening at the height of summer, as I prepared to

leave him for the night, he put out his hand and touched mine. 'Thank y', lad,' he said in a voice grown very tired and weak. 'An' he'll not forget what I've told him?'

I was suddenly very moved; a lump came into my throat. 'No, Grandad,' I told him, 'I'll not forget.'

He gently patted my hand, then looked away and closed his eyes. The next morning my mother told me that he had died in his sleep.

They laid him out in the damp mustiness of his own front room, among the tasselled chairback covers and the lustres under their thin glass domes; and they let me see him for a moment. I did not stay long with him. He looked little different from the scores of times I had seen him during his illness, except that his fretting hands were stilled beneath the sheet and his hair and moustache had the inhuman antiseptic cleanliness of death. Afterwards, in the quiet of my own room, I cried a little, remembering that I should see him no more, and that I had talked with him and read to him for the last time.

After the funeral the family descended upon us in force for the reading of the will. There was not much to quarrel about: my grandfather had never made much money, and what little he left had been saved slowly, thriftily over the years. It was divided fairly evenly along with the value of the house, the only condition being that the house was not to be sold, but that my mother was to be allowed to live in it and take part of her livelihood from Grandfather's smallholding (which she had in fact managed during his illness) for as long as she liked, or until she married again, which was not likely, since no one knew whether my father was alive or dead.

It was when they reached the personal effects that we got a surprise, for my grandfather had left his watch to me!

'Why your Will?' my Uncle Henry asked in surly tones. 'I've two lads o' me own and both older than Will.'

'An' neither of 'em ever seemed to know their grandfather was poorly,' my mother retorted, sharp as a knife.

'Young an' old don't mix,' Uncle Henry muttered, and my mother, thoroughly ruffled, snapped back, 'Well Will an' his grandfather mixed very nicely, and your father was right glad of his company when there wasn't so much of anybody else's.'

This shot got home on Uncle Henry, who had been a poor sick-visitor. It never took my family long to work up a row and listening from the kitchen through the partly open door, I waited for some real north-country family sparring. But my Uncle John, Grandfather's eldest son, and a fair man, chipped in and put a stop to it. 'Now that's enough,' he rumbled in his deep voice. 'We'll have no wranglin' wi' the old man hardly in his coffin.' There was a short pause and I could imagine him looking round at everyone. 'I'd a fancy for that watch meself, but me father knew what he was about an' if he chose to leave it young Will, then I'm not goin' to argue about it.' And that was the end of it; the watch was mine.

The house seemed very strange without my grandfather and during the half-hour after tea, when it had been my custom to sit with him, I felt for a long time greatly at a loss. The watch had a lot to do with this feeling. I still admired it in the late afternoon but now it hung by the mantelshelf in the kitchen where I had persuaded my mother to let it be. My grandfather and his watch had always been inseparable in my mind, and to see the watch without at the same time seeing him was to feel keenly the awful finality of his going. The new position of the watch was in the nature of a compromise between my mother and me. While it was officially mine, it was being held in trust by my mother until she considered me old enough and careful enough to look after it. She was all for putting it away till that time, but I protested so strongly that she finally agreed to keep it in the kitchen where I could see it all the time, taking care, however, to have it away in a drawer when any of the family were expected, because, she said, there was no point in 'rubbing it in.'

The holidays came to an end and it was time for me to start my first term at the Grammar School in Cressley. A host of new excitements came to fill my days. I was cast into the melting pot of the first form and I had to work for my position in that new fraternity along with twenty-odd other boys from all parts of the town. Friendships were made in those first weeks which would last into adult life. One formed first opinions about one's fellows, and one had one's own label stuck on according to the first impression made. For first impressions seemed vital, and it looked as though the boy who was lucky or clever enough to assert himself favourably at the start would have an advantage for the rest of his schooldays.

There are many ways in which a boy—or a man—may try to establish himself with his fellows. One or two of my classmates grovelled at everyone's feet, while others took the opposite line and tried systematically to beat the form into submission, starting with the smallest boy and working up till they met their match. Others charmed everyone by their skill at sports, and others by simply being themselves and seeming hardly to make any effort at all. I have never made friends easily and I was soon branded as aloof. For a time I did little more than get on speaking terms with my fellows.

One of our number was the youngest son of a well-to-do local tradesman and he had a brother who was a prefect in the sixth. His way of asserting himself was to parade his possessions before our envious eyes; and while these tactics did not win him popularity they gained him a certain following and made him one of the most discussed members of the form. Crawley's bicycle was brand new and had a three-speed gear, an oil-bath gearcase, a speedometer, and other desirable refinements. Crawley's fountain pen matched his propelling pencil and had a gold nib. His football boots were of the best hide and his gym slippers were reinforced with rubber across the toes. Everything, in fact, that Crawley had was better than ours. Until he brought the watch.

He flashed it on his wrist with arrogant pride, making a great show of looking at the time. His eldest brother had brought it from abroad. He'd even smuggled it through the customs especially for him. Oh, yes, said Crawley, it had a sweep second-hand and luminous figures, and wasn't it absolutely the finest watch we had ever seen? But I was thinking of my grandfather's watch: *my* watch now. There had never been a watch to compare with that. With heart-thumping excitement I found myself cutting in on Crawley's self-satisfied eulogy.

'I've seen a better watch than that.'

'Gerraway!'

'Yes I have,' I insisted. 'It was my grandfather's. He left it to me when he died.'

'Well show us it,' Crawley said.

'I haven't got it here.'

'You haven't got it at all,' Crawley said. 'You can't show us it to prove it.'

I could have knocked the sneer from his hateful face

in rage that he could doubt the worth of the watch for which my grandfather had worked fifty years.

'I'll bring it this afternoon,' I said; 'then you'll see!'

The hand of friendship was extended tentatively in my direction several times that morning. I should not be alone in my pleasure at seeing Crawley taken down a peg. As the clock moved with maddening slowness to half-past twelve I thought with grim glee of how in one move I would settle Crawley's boasting and assert myself with my fellows. On the bus going home, however, I began to wonder how on earth I was going to persuade my mother to let me take the watch out of doors. But I had forgotten that today was Monday, washing day, when my mother put my grandfather's watch in a drawer, away from the steam. I had only to wait for her to step outside for a moment and I could slip the watch into my pocket. She would not miss it before I came home for tea. And if she did, it would be too late.

I was too eager and excited to wait for the return bus and after dinner I got my bike out of the shed. My mother watched me from the kitchen doorway and I could imagine her keen eyes piercing the cloth of my blazer to where the watch rested guiltily in my pocket.

'Are you going on your bike, then, Will?'

I said, 'Yes, Mother,' and, feeling uncomfortable under that direct gaze, began to wheel the bike across the yard.

'I thought you said it needed mending or something before you rode it again . . .?'

'It's only a little thing,' I told her. 'It'll be all right.'

I waved good-bye and pedalled out into the street while she watched me, a little doubtfully, I thought. Once out of sight of the house I put all my strength on the pedals and rode like the wind. My grandfather's house was in one of the older parts of the town and my way led through a maze of steep cobbled streets between long rows of houses. I kept up my speed, excitement coursing through me as I thought of the watch and revelled in my hatred of Crawley. Then from an entry between two terraces of houses a mongrel puppy darted into the street. I pulled at my back brake. The cable snapped with a click – that was what I had intended to fix. I jammed on the front brake with the puppy cowering foolishly in my path. The bike jarred to a standstill, the back end swinging as though catapulted over the pivot of the stationary front wheel, and I went over the handlebars.

A man picked me up out of the gutter. 'All right, lad?'

I nodded uncertainly. I seemed unhurt. I rubbed my knees and the side on which I had fallen. I felt the outline of the watch. Sick apprehension overcame me, but I waited till I was round the next corner before dismounting again and putting a trembling hand into my pocket. Then I looked down at what was left of my grandfather's proudest possession. There was a deep bulge in the back of the case. The glass was shattered and the Roman numerals looked crazily at one another across the pierced and distorted face. I put the watch back in my pocket and rode slowly on, my mind numb with misery.

I thought of showing them what was left; but that was no use. I had promised them a prince among watches and no amount of beautiful wreckage would do.

'Where's the watch, Will?' they asked. 'Have you brought the watch?'

'My mother wouldn't let me bring it,' I lied, moving to my desk, my hand in my pocket clutching the shattered watch.

'His mother wouldn't let him,' Crawley jeered. 'What a tale!'

(Later, Crawley, I thought. The day will come.)

The others took up his cries. I was branded as a romancer, a fanciful liar. I couldn't blame them after letting them down.

The bell rang for first class and I sat quietly at my desk, waiting for the master to arrive. I opened my books and stared blindly at them as a strange feeling stole over me. It was not the mocking of my classmates—they would tire of that eventually. Nor was it the thought of my mother's anger, terrible though that would be. No, all I could think of – all that possessed my mind – was the old man, my grandfather, lying in his bed after a long life of toil, his hands fretting with the sheets, and his tired, breathy voice saying, 'Patience, Will, patience.'

And I nearly wept, for it was the saddest moment of my young life.

A LOVELY VIEW OF THE GASWORKS

'WELL,' he said after a silence, 'what d'you think to it?'

She answered him from the tall sash window where for several minutes she had been standing gazing out across the town in a dreamy, pre-occupied sort of way. 'Lovely view of the gasworks,' she said, stirring now and rubbing slowly at her bare upper arm with her left hand.

He had been keenly aware of her absorption of mind ever since meeting her that evening and it had created uneasiness in him. Now he said, with the suggestion of an edge to his voice, 'It doesn't matter what's outside; it's what's inside 'at counts,' and some deeper significance in his words made her glance sharply at him and seemed to bring her back from wherever her thoughts had carried her to the room and him.

'D'you think it might be damp?' she said, rubbing gently now at both arms together. 'It's none too warm in here.'

'The sun's gone,' the man said. 'And the house has been empty for weeks. You'd soon notice a difference when we'd had fires going a bit.'

She was quick to notice his choice of words, as though he himself had already accepted the house and now awaited only her acquiescence for the matter to be settled.

'You're a bit set on it, aren't you?' she said, watching him.

'I don't think it's bad,' he said, pursing his lips in the

way she knew so well. 'I've seen plenty worse. Course, I've seen plenty better an' all, but it's no use crying after the moon.'

'It seems all right,' she said, looking round the bed-room. And now, strangely enough, it looked less all right than it had when they first came in. Then, lit by the evening sun, this room in particular had seemed charm-ingly airy and bright; but now the sun had gone she could see only the shabbiness of the faded blue wallpaper and feel how bleakly empty it was. She paced away from the window, a dark girl with a sallow complexion and pale bloodless lips, wearing a home-made yellow frock which hung loosely on her bony body. And suddenly then all the feeling the man had previously sensed in her seemed to burst and flood out as her features lost their control, and she threw up her hands.

'Oh, I don't know,' she cried. 'I don't know if it's worth it or not.'

'You mean the house?' he said, hoping she did, but knowing more.

'All of it,' she said with passion. 'Everything.' And she turned her face from him.

As he watched her his own face seemed to sag into lines of hopelessness and his nostrils quivered in a heavy sigh. 'I didn't think you'd come,' he said. 'I didn't think you'd do it in the end.'

'I haven't said I won't, have I?' she snapped over her shoulder.

'Well what's wrong, then?' he said. 'What is it?'

'It's her,' the girl said. 'I saw her this afternoon. She followed me all round town. Everywhere I went, she followed. I thought about stopping and giving her a piece of my mind, but I knew she wouldn't mind a scene.'

'You did right not to speak to her. She enjoys feeling badly done to. She always did. God!' he said with feeling. 'Why can't she leave us alone? She gets her money reg'lar, doesn't she? What more does she want?'

'You,' the girl said, turning to look at him.

'She never wanted me when she had me,' he said. 'A home, kids, the sort o' things everybody gets married for —she never wanted any o' them things.'

'You don't know much about women, do you?' the girl said.

'Not a thing. Not one damn thing.'

'She's your wife,' the girl said. 'And that's more than I'll ever be.'

She was near to tears now and he crossed the bare floorboards between them to take her in his arms and draw her to him.

'I'd marry you tomorrow. You know that.'

'I know, I know. But she'll never set you free.'

'Who knows?' he said past her shoulder. 'One day, p'raps.'

'And till then?'

'That's up to you. You're the one with everything to lose. You've your people to face, an' your friends. Folk'll talk three times as much about you as me. They won't blame me: they'll blame you. They'll say you're a fool for risking everything for a bloke like me. They'll say I can't be much good anyway: I couldn't keep steady with a woman when I was wed to her, so what chance have you to hold me without even your marriage lines. They'll tell you I could leave you flat any time and you'd have no claim on me. *She's* got all the claims. You'll have nothing.'

'Oh, stop it,' she said. 'Stop it.'

He turned away from her and felt for his cigarettes. The packet was empty and he crushed it and hurled it into the fireplace.

'Who the hell am I to ask you to do this?' he said. 'You could be lookin' round for some lad your own age. Somebody 'at could marry you, all decent an' above board.'

She looked at him, thinking how different love was from the way she had always imagined it would be, and she came again to the verge of tears before his thin balding figure in the ill-fitting sports coat and creased flannel trousers, and the baffled way he took life's blows on the face.

She ran and clung to him. 'I want you to ask me,' she said; 'because I want you. I want to give you peace and love and a home, and, someday, kids. Everything a man should have from a woman. Everything you've never had in your life.'

'You're a grand kid,' he said, stroking her hair. 'So sweet and good and grand. I keep telling myself, if only I'd met you earlier; and then I remember that you were only a nipper then. You're not much more now really.'

'I'll be all the woman you'll ever want,' she said fiercely, clinging to him. 'You'll see.'

They came apart with a start as the woman's voice hailed them from the foot of the stairs. 'Hello, are you there?'

The man crossed the room to the door and called down, 'Yes, we're just coming.'

He looked back at the girl and she joined him at the head of the uncarpeted stairs. They went down, the girl twisting the signet ring on the third finger of her left hand, to where the woman was standing in the living-room.

'Well,' she said, watching them keenly, her hands folded under her clean pinafore, 'have you seen everything?'

'I think so,' the man said.

'It seems very nice,' the girl said.

'It's not a palace,' the woman said bluntly; 'but of course, you're not looking for a palace, eh?'

'No,' they said, and smiled.

'Six hundred, you said, didn't you?' the man asked.

'Six hundred cash,' the woman said. 'Six-fifty otherwise.'

'Oh, we'd pay cash, but we'd have to see about a mortgage first.'

'No need to do that,' the woman said briskly. 'That's what I mean by otherwise. My solicitor can draw up an agreement. You pay me a hundred and fifty down and the rest at thirty shillings a week. That's fair enough, isn't it?'

'I think that's very decent,' the man said. 'We were a bit worried about the building society. They're getting very choosy about their loans nowadays.'

'Aye, and putting their interest rates up every other week,' the woman said. 'Well, we've no need to bring them into it at all. I'm selling all my houses the same way. It gives me a bit of capital and a regular income. That's my offer, and you won't get a better anywhere else.'

'I'm sure we won't,' the girl said, and she and the man exchanged glances.

The man said, 'We'll have to talk it over.'

'Yes, have a talk about it. But don't wait too long if you want it. Would this be your first home?'

'Yes, the first.'

'With your in-laws now, is that it?'

'Yes, that's right,' the man said, and the girl found

herself wondering what change there would be in the woman's brisk friendliness were she to tell her that he had left his wife and they wanted somewhere to live in sin. She thought it would come out eventually anyway. You wouldn't hide much from this woman for long.

'Well you think it over,' the woman said, moving across to the door.

'Yes, we'll let you know either way,' the man said.

Walking away from the house, up the long street, the girl with her arm through his, the man seemed suddenly full of hope and high spirits. 'Just right,' he said. 'Not too big, and no messing about with building societies. That's a stroke of luck. I think I know where to scrape up the deposit, and we'll manage nicely after that.' He squeezed her arm. 'Just imagine,' he said, 'living there together all nice and snug. All our troubles'll be over then.'

How easy, she thought, for her to dim the optimism in his voice and extinguish the bright hope on his face. She shuddered as she felt the shadow of a third person walking between them. But echoing his eager tones, she said, 'Yes, all our troubles'll be over then,' while in her heart she wondered if after all they might be only just beginning.

'GAMBLERS NEVER WIN'

In the dusk of the winter afternoon Mrs Scurridge stirred from her nap by the fire as she heard the light movements of her husband in the bedroom overhead, and she was already on her feet in the firelight and filling the soot-grimed copper kettle at the sink when he came into the big farmhouse kitchen, his thin dark hair tangled on his narrow skull, his sharp-featured face unshaven, and blurred with Saturday-afternoon sleep. He crossed the room to the fireplace without a word or a glance for her and ran his hand along the mantelshelf in search of a cigarette-end. He wore a striped flannel shirt, without collar, the sleeves rolled up above his elbows, and over it an unbuttoned navy blue waistcoat. Besides braces he wore a heavy leather belt buckled loosely about his thin waist. He was a shortish, bandy-legged man and he had to stretch up on his toes to bring his eyes level with the mantelshelf. After a moment's fumbling he found the partly smoked Woodbine and pushed a twist of paper into the fire to get a light. The first mouthful of smoke started him coughing and he was helpless for some moments, bending over and supporting himself by the palm of his hand on the tall, old-fashioned fireplace while the phlegm cracked and gurgled in his throat. When the attack had passed he spat into the fire, straightened up, wiping the spittle from his thin lips with the back of his hand, and spoke:

'Tea ready?'

His wife pushed him aside and put the kettle on the fire, pressing it firmly down on the glowing coals.

'It can be,' she said, 'as soon as you know what you want.'

She picked up the twist of paper that Scurridge had dropped in the hearth and lit the single gas mantle suspended directly over the table. The gas popped and flared, then settled down to a dim, miserable glow which revealed the heartbreaking shabbiness of the room: the square table with bulbous legs hacked and scarred by years of careless feet; the sagging chairs with their bulging springs and worn and dirty upholstery; the thin, cracked linoleum on the broad expanse of damp, stone-flagged floor; and the great brown patch of damp on the wall—as though someone had spilt a potful of coffee against the grimy wallpaper – in one corner of the room. The very atmosphere was permeated with the musty odour of damp decay, an odour which no amount of fire could drive from the house.

Scurridge reached for the morning newspaper and turned to the sports page. 'I fancy a bit o' bacon an' egg,' he said, and sat down beside the fire and placed his pointed elbows in the centres of the two threadbare patches on the arms of his chair.

His wife threw a surly glance at the upraised newspaper. 'There is no eggs,' she said, and Scurridge's pale, watery blue eyes fixed on her for the first time as he lowered the paper.

'What y' mean "there is no eggs"?'

'I mean what I say; I didn't get any.' She added with sullen defiance, 'I couldn't afford 'em this week. They're five-an'-six a dozen. Something's got to go – I can't buy all I should as it is.'

Scurridge smacked his lips peevishly. 'God! Oh! God. Are we at it again? It's one bloody thing after the other. I don't know what you do with your brass.'

'I spend it on keeping you,' she said. 'God knows *I* get precious little out of it. Always a good table, you must have. Never anything short. Anybody 'ud think you'd never heard of the cost of living. I've told you time an' again 'at it isn't enough, but it makes no difference.'

'Didn't I give you another half-crown on'y the other week?' Scurridge demanded, sitting forward in his chair. 'Didn't I? It's about time you knew how to spend your brass; you've been housekeepin' long enough.'

She knew the hopelessness of further argument and took refuge, as always, behind the bulwark of her apathy. She lit the gas-ring and put on the frying pan. 'You can have some fried bread with your bacon,' she said. 'Will that do?'

'I reckon it'll have to do, won't it?' Scurridge said.

She turned on the upraised newspaper a look in which there was nothing of hatred or malice or rebellion, but only a dull, flat apathy, an almost unfeeling acceptance of the facts of her life, against which she only now and again raised her voice in a token protest; because, after all, she was still capable, however remotely, of comparing them with what might have been.

She laid a place for Scurridge on a newspaper at one corner of the table and while he ate there she sat huddled to the fire, nibbling at a slice of bread and jam, her left hand holding the fold of her overall close over her flaccid breasts. The skin of her face was sallow and pouchy; her hair, dark and without lustre, was drawn back in a lank sweep and knotted untidily on the nape of her neck. Her legs, once her best feature, were swollen in places with ugly blue veins. Only in her eyes, almost black, was the prettiness of her youth ever revealed, and this only momentarily when they flashed in an anger now rare. For most of the time they were like dark windows on to a soul lost in an unmindful trance. Little more than forty-five years old, she had become already worn and aged before her time in the unending struggle of her life with Scurridge in this bleak and cheerless house which stood alone on a hillside above Cressley, an eternity from lights and noise and the warmth of human laughter.

Scurridge pushed away his plate and ran his tongue across his greasy lips. He drank the last of his tea and set the pint mug down on the table. 'Been better wi' an egg,' he said. His forefinger groped into his waistcoat pocket, searching absently for another cigarette-end. 'You want to economise,' he said. He smacked his lips, seeming to savour the word along with the fat from the bread. 'Economise,' he said again.

'What on?' his wife asked wearily, without hope of a reasonable answer. She had been whittling down her own needs for years, pruning where he would feel it least, and now there were only the bare necessities left for her to give up. It was a long time since any little luxuries had cushioned the hard edges of her existence.

'How the hell should I know?' Scurridge said. 'It's not my job to know, is it? I've done my whack when I've worked an' earned the brass.'

'Aye, an' spent it.'

'Aye, an' haven't I a right to a bit o' pleasure when I've slaved me guts out all week, eh? An' how do other folk manage, eh? There's many a woman 'ud be glad o' what I give you.' He got up to search on the mantelshelf once more.

'Nine out o'ten women 'ud throw it back in your face.'

'Oh, aye,' Scurridge said, 'I know you think you're badly done to. You allus have. But I know how t'men talk in t'pit an' happen you're better off than you think.'

She said nothing, but her mind was disturbingly alive. Oh! God, he hadn't always been like this: not at first: only since that demon had got into him, that demon of lust, lust for easy money and a life of idleness. She had never known the exact amount of his wages but she had once caught a glimpse of a postal order he had bought to send off with his football pools and the amount on it had horrified her, representing as it did the senseless throwing away of a comfortable, decent life.

As Scurridge straightened up from lighting his cigarette he peered at her, his eyes focusing with unaccustomed attention on one particular feature of her. 'What you done wi' your hand?' he said. He spoke roughly, without warmth, as though fearing some trap of sentiment she had laid for him.

'I caught meself on the clothes-line hook in the back wall.' Mrs Scurridge said. 'It's rusty an' sharp as a needle.' She looked vaguely down at the rough bandage and said without emotion, 'I shouldn't be surprised if it turns to blood poisoning.'

He turned away, muttering. 'Aw, you allus make the worst of anythin'.'

'Well, it's not the first time I've done it,' she told him. 'If you'd put me another post up I shouldn't have to use it.'

'Aye, if I put you another post up,' Scurridge sneered. 'If I did this, that an' the other thing. Is there owt else you want while we're at it?'

Goaded, she flung out her arm and pointed to the great stain of damp in the corner. 'There's that! And half the windows won't shut properly. It's time you did summat about the place before it tumbles round your ears!'

'Jesus Christ and God Almighty,' Scurridge said. 'Can't I have any peace? Haven't I done enough when I've sweated down yon' hole wi'out startin' again when I get home?' He picked up his paper. 'Besides, it all costs brass.'

'Aye, it all costs brass. The hens cost brass so you killed 'em all off by one and now you can't have any eggs. The garden cost brass so you let it turn into a wilderness. The sheds cost brass so now they're all mouldering away out there. We could have had a nice little small holding to keep us when you came out of the pit; but no, it all costs brass, so now we've got nothing.'

He rustled the paper and spoke from behind it. 'We'd never ha' made it pay. This place 'ud run away wi' every penny if I let it.'

The mad injustice of it tore at her long-nurtured patience and it was, for a moment of temper, more than she could bear. 'Better than it all going on beer an' pools an' dog-racing,' she flared. 'Making bookies an' publicans their bellies fat.'

'You think I'm a blasted fool, don't you? You think I'm just throwin' good money after bad?' His hands crushed the edges of the newspaper and the demon glared malevolently at her from his weak blue eyes. 'You don't see 'at I'm out for a further fetch. There'll be a killin' one o'these days. It's got to come. The whole bloody kitty 'ull drop into me lap an' then I'll be laughin'.'

She turned her face from the stare of the demon and muttered, 'Gambling's a sin.' She did not really believe this and she felt with the inadequacy of the retort surprise that she should have uttered those words. They were not her own but her father's and she wondered that she should clutch at the tatters of his teaching after all this time.

'Don't mouth that old hypocrite's words at me,' Scurridge said without heat.

'Don't tell you anything, eh?' she said. 'You know it all, I reckon? That's why your own daughter left home – because you 'at knew it all drove her away. Well mind you don't do the same with me!'

This brought him leaping from his chair to stand over her, his face working with fury. 'Don't talk about her in this house,' he shouted. 'Damned ungrateful bitch! I don't want to hear owt about her, d'you hear?' He reeled away as the cough erupted into his throat and he crouched by the fire until the attack had passed, drawing great wheezing gulps of air. 'An' if you want to go,' he said, 'you can get off any time you're ready.'

She knew he did not mean this. She knew also that she would never go. She had never seriously considered it. Eva, on her furtive visits to the house while her father was out, had often asked her how she stood it; but she knew she would never leave him. Over the years she had found herself thinking back more and more to her father and she was coming now to accept her life as the inevitable consequence, as predicted by him, of the lapse into the

sin which had bound her to Scurridge and brought Eva
into the world. Eva who, as the wheel turned full circle,
had departed without blessing from *her* father's house,
though for a different reason. No, she would never leave
him. But neither could she foresee any future with him
as she was. She had come to believe in the truth of her
father's prediction that nothing good would come of their
life together and she was sometimes haunted by an
elusive though disturbing sense of impending tragedy.
The day was long past when she could hope for a
return to sanity of Scurridge. He was too far gone now:
the demon was too securely a part of him. But she too
had passed the point of no return. For good or for bad,
this was her life, and she could not run away from life
itself.

They sat on before the fire, two intimate strangers,
with nothing more to say to each other; and about six
o'clock Scurridge got up from his chair and washed and
shaved sketchily in the sink in the corner. She looked up
dully as he prepared to take his leave.

'Dogs?' she said.

'It's Saturday, in't it?' Scurridge answered, pulling on
his overcoat.

All the loneliness of the evening seemed to descend upon
her at once then and she said with the suggestion of a
whine in her voice, 'Why don't you take me with you some
Saturday?'

'You?' he said. 'Take you? D'you think you're fit to
take anywhere? Look at yersen! An' when I think of
you as you used to be!'

She looked away. The abuse had little sting now.
She could think of him too, as he used to be; but she
did not do that too often now, for such memories had

the power of evoking a misery which was stronger than the inertia that, over the years, had become her only defence.

'What time will you be back?'

'Expect me when you see me,' he said at the door. 'Is'll want a bite o' supper, I expect.'

Expect him at whatever time his tipsy legs brought him home, she thought. If he lost he would drink to console himself. If he won he would drink to celebrate. Either way there was nothing in it for her but yet more ill temper, yet further abuse.

She got up a few minutes after he had gone and went to the back door to look out. It was snowing again and the clean, gentle fall softened the stark and ugly outlines of the decaying outhouses on the patch of land behind the house and gently obliterated Scurridge's footprints where they led away from the door, down the slope to the wood, through which ran a path to the main road, a mile distant. She shivered as the cold air touched her, and returned indoors, beginning, despite herself, to remember. Once the sheds had been sound and strong and housed poultry. The garden had flourished too, supplying them with sufficient vegetables for their own needs and some left to sell. Now it was overgrown with rampant grass and dock. And the house itself – they had bought it for a song because it was old and really too big for one woman to manage; but it too had been strong and sound and it had looked well under regular coats of paint and with the walls pointed and the windows properly hung. In the early days, seeing it all begin to slip from her grasp, she had tried to keep it going herself. But it was a thankless, hopeless struggle without support from Scurridge: a struggle which had beaten her in the end, driving her first into frustration and then finally apathy. Now everything was mouldering and dilapidated and its gradual decay was like a symbol of her own decline from the hopeful young wife and mother into the tired old woman she was now.

Listlessly she washed up and put away the teapots. Then she took the coal-bucket from the hearth and went down into the dripping, dungeon-like darkness of the huge cellar. There she filled the bucket and lugged it back up the steps. Mending the fire, piling it high with the wet gleaming lumps of coal, she drew some comfort from the fact that this at least, with Scurridge's miner's allocation, was one thing of which they were never short. This job done, she switched on the battery-fed wireless set and stretched out her feet in their torn canvas shoes to the blaze.

They were broadcasting a programme of old-time dance music: the Lancers, the Barn Dance, the Veleta. *You are my honey-honey-suckle, I am the bee* . . . Both she and Scurridge had loved old-time dancing a long time, a long long time ago; and, scorning the modern fox-trots, how often they had danced so in the first years of marriage while some kind friend looked to the baby, Eva! Oh, those wonderful early days: that brief era of glorious freedom, with the narrow restrictions of her father's house behind her and the mad decline of Scurridge in the unknown future! Oh! those times . . . There seemed to be a conspiracy afoot tonight, set on making her remember, and she sat there while the radio played, letting the old tunes wash the long-submerged memories on to the shores of her mind; and later on she took a candle and went up into the cold, barn-like bedroom and climbing on a chair, rummaged in a cupboard over the built-in wardrobe and eventually unearthed a photograph album. Rubbing the mildewed cover on her overall, she took the album down to her chair by the fire. It was years since she had looked into the album and slowly now she turned the pages and went back across the years to her youth.

She was asleep when the knock came at the back door to startle her into sudden wakefulness, and consciousness that the gaslight had failed and the room was lit only by the flicker of the big fire in the grate. She thought for a bemused moment that she had imagined the sound, and then it was repeated, more insistently this time, and she got up and after picking up and placing on the table the photograph album which had slid from her knee while she dozed, went into the passage.

She stood a few feet from the door and called out, 'Who is it? Who's there?' It was a lonely house and, though she was not normally nervous, being awakened so abruptly had disturbed her a little.

'It's me,' a woman's voice answered; 'Eva.'

'Oh!' Mrs Scurridge stepped forward and unbolted the door and swung it open. 'Come in, love, come in. I wasn't expecting you tonight. You must be near frozen through.'

'Just a minute,' her daughter said. 'I'll just give Eric a shout.' She walked to the corner of the house and called out. A man's voice answered her and then there was the coughing splutter of a motor-cycle engine from the road at the front of the house.

'I thought you mustn't be in when I couldn't see a light,' Eva said when she came back. She kicked the snow off her boots against the step before coming into the passage.

'What're you doing sitting in the dark? Don't tell me you haven't a penny for the gas now.'

'It went out while I was having a little nap.' They went along the stone-flagged passage and into the fire-lit kitchen. 'I'll just find me purse and see if I've any coppers.'

'No, here.' Eva took out her own purse. 'I've a shilling here: that'll last longer.'

'Well, I've got some coppers . . .' her mother began; but Eva had already crossed the room and her heels were clacking on the steps to the cellar. Mrs Scurridge put a twist of paper into the fire and when she heard the shilling fall in the meter, lit the gas-mantle.

'Isn't Eric comin' in, then?' she asked as Eva returned.

'He's got a football club meeting in Cressley,' Eva said. 'He's callin' back for me. He might pop in for a minute then.'

Her mother watched her as she took off her headscarf and gingerly fingered her newly permed mouse-brown hair.

'A busy young man, your Eric.'

'Oh, here, there an' everywhere.' Eva took off her heavy tweed coat. Under it she had on a dark green wool dress. Round the high neck of the dress she was wearing a necklace of an imitation gold finish with a matching bracelet round her wrist. She brought an air of comfortable prosperity and well-being with her in the shabby room.

'They made him a foreman at the Works last week,' she said, with a faint note of complacent pride in her voice.

'Ah, promotion, eh?'

Eva lifted her skirt from the hips to avoid 'seating' it

and sat down in her father's chair. She levered off her fur-lined winter boots and put her nylon-stockinged feet on the kerb. 'He'll be manager one day,' she said. 'Everybody says how clever he is.'

'Well, it's nice to hear of a young man getting on,' her mother said; 'especially when he's something to you.'

Eva ran her palms up and down her calves then pushed back the hem of her skirt to expose her knees to the fire. She was a thin young woman, easily chilled, and she could not remember ever being able to keep warm in this house in winter. She stretched out her hands and leaned towards the blaze.

'Brrrh! What weather . . . It's freezing like anything outside.'

'I hope your Eric'll be safe on his bike.'

'Oh, he'll be all right. He's a careful driver; and it's better with the sidecar on, weather like this . . . Have you been cutting yourself?' she asked, noticing her mother's hand for the first time.

Mrs Scurridge told her what had happened and Eva said, 'You want to look after it. Don't let it turn septic.'

Mrs Scurridge dismissed the injury with a shrug. 'It's only a scratch. I've put some salve on it. It'll heal up in a day or two . . .

'I like your frock,' she said after a moment. 'Is it new?'

'Well, nearly. I've only worn it two or three times. I got it in Leeds when we were looking at furniture. It was in Creston's window – y'know, in Briggate – an' it took me eye straight away. Eric saw me looking at it an' he bought it me. I knew we couldn't afford it, what with all the expense of movin' an' everything, but he talked me into it.' She gave a short laugh of feminine pleasure at this thought of her husband's indulgence.

'You've got moved and everything, then?'

'Yes, we're in, thank the Lord. It'll take a bit of making comfortable, what with it being so new an' all that, but it's like heaven after livin' in digs.'

'I dare say it will be. But you got on all right with the folk you lodged with, didn't you? You never had any trouble or anything?'

'Oh, no, nothing like that. Not that there hasn't been times when I could have said a thing or two, mind. But Mrs Walshaw's much too reserved an' ladylike to ever have words with anybody. She had a way of looking down her nose at you 'at I never liked. She'd taken quite a fancy to Eric, y'know, what with her an' Mr Walshaw not havin' any child of their own, an' I believe she thought he'd never find a lass good enough for him. No, you can't quarrel with Mrs Walshaw. Quite the lady, she is. You'd never think to meet her she'd made all her money keepin' a fish and chip shop an' taking lodgers in.'

'Aye, it takes all sorts . . . You'll have been kept busy for a bit, then?'

'Oh, you've no idea. What with cleanin' an' paintin' and buying furniture an' making curtains, we've had a real month of it. But it's such a lovely house, Mother. I walk round sometimes when Eric's at work and tell meself it's really ours. An' I still can't believe it. I'm always thinkin' I'll wake up one morning and find we're back in Mrs Walshaw's back bedroom.'

There was a short silence while Eva gently rubbed her legs in the heat of the fire. Then Mrs Scurridge said diffidently, 'You're not . . . You don't think you're over-reaching yourselves at all, do you? You know what I mean: taking on a bit more than you can manage.'

'Oh, no,' Eva said; 'we're all right. We've been saving up ever since we were married. Both of us working. An' Eric was always careful as a single lad, y'know. He never threw his money around like a lot of 'em do. No, we'll be all right. We shall have to pull our horns in a bit from now on; but we'll manage nicely, thank you.'

'Well then,' said her mother, satisfied. 'You know your own know best. An' I'm right glad 'at you're settled in a home of your own at last.'

'An' you can come an' see us any time you like now,' Eva said. 'It's not far – just half an hour on the bus from Cressley.'

'Yes, I'll have to see about it now. I'll be poppin' over one o' these fine days. Just let's get a bit o' better weather here.'

Eva toasted her knees. 'Well,' she said, 'an' how are you keeping?'

Mrs Scurridge gave a faint shrug. 'Oh, so so. A touch of lumbago now an' again; but I can't grumble. I'll be happier when we have a bit better weather. You feel so cut off here when there's snow on the ground. Half a mile from the nearest house and hardly any traffic on the road at night.'

'You should get out more,' Eva said, ' 'stead o' sittin' in night after night.'

'Aye, I suppose I should. You get out of the habit, though. And besides, this weather—'

'No need to ask about me father,' Eva said. 'Seems this weather doesn't keep him in. Where's he gone tonight? Down town?'

Her mother nodded, looking into the fire. 'Dogs, I suppose.'

'Leaving you here on your own, as usual.'

'There's no pleasure out on a night like this.'

Eva nodded. 'I know all about it.' She drew in her breath. 'I don't know how you stand it. I don't, honestly.' Her gaze flickered round the room and the dinginess of what she saw seemed so to oppress her that she barely restrained a shudder. 'Thank God I got out when I had the chance.'

'It was different with you,' her mother said. 'You'd have gone anyway, sometime.'

'Not if *he'd* had his way. It just suited his book having *two* women about the house to wait on him. An' with my money coming in he could hang on to more of his own.' She stopped, then burst out in angry impatience, 'I don't see it. I just don't see it. A husband should be somebody like Eric, who considers his wife an' looks after her. An' when he stops being like that your duty stops as well. You don't owe me father a thing. You could walk out of here tonight an' nobody could blame you. An' you know there's a place waiting for you any time you want it now. You've somewhere to go now.'

Mrs Scurridge threw a shrewd glance at her daughter's profile, flushed pink now from the heat of the fire and her outburst of indignation. 'Is that what Eric thinks too?' she said. 'What does he think about it?'

'Well . . . he thinks like I do. He doesn't know why you stick it.'

'But that doesn't mean he'd be happy to be saddled with his mother-in-law as soon as he's settled in his first home. Especially a mother-in-law like me.'

'Why especially like you?'

'Well, I don't suppose he thinks I'm the smartest woman he's ever seen.'

'But you *could* be smart,' Eva cried. 'You could if you

got away from here. What's the use of bothering here, though, livin' week in an' week out miles from anywhere with a husband who spends all his money on gamblin' an' drinkin'? How can anybody take a pride in conditions like that?'

'Well, my place is with your father, Eva, and that's all there is to it.'

'But you don't—'

'That'll do,' her mother said quietly.

Eva said, 'Oh!' and stood up with an impatient gesture. The radio was still playing. 'Do we have to have this thing on?'

'You can switch it off if you like. I was listening to some old-time dance music, but it's over now.'

Eva went round the back of the chair and turned the knob. In the silence that followed she remained standing there, one hand resting on top of the wireless cabinet, her back to her mother.

'Mother,' she said suddenly, and turned round, 'am I illegitimate?'

Her mother started. 'No, you're not.'

'But you an' me dad had to get married because of me, hadn't you?'

'No, no. It wasn't quite like that. We did get married when we knew you were coming; but we should have done anyway. We weren't forced into it.' She met her daughter's eyes. 'How did you find out?'

'Oh, it's something I've had in the back of me mind for a long while now,' Eva said, still standing behind the chair. 'It was just a matter of checkin' a couple of dates to make sure.'

'Have you said anything to Eric?'

'No.'

'Are you going to?'

'I don't see why I should.'

'Neither do I,' Mrs Scurridge said. 'But you don't think he'd mind, do you?'

'I don't know,' Eva said frankly. 'He . . . Well, he's a bit straitlaced about some things, is Eric. I don't see any point in spoiling anything . . .'

'But nobody can call you illegitimate, Eva,' Mrs Scurridge said. 'We were married months before y . . .' She turned her gaze to the fire. 'I'm sorry, love. I never saw any reason to tell you.'

'Oh, don't *you* be sorry.' Eva's mouth set. 'It's him, not you.'

'You shouldn't hate your father so much, Eva.'

'How can I help it when everything he touches turns rotten? He's spoilt your life an' he'd have done the same with mine if I hadn't stood up to him. He couldn't even get married in a right way. He had to get hold of you by getting you into trouble.'

'It wasn't like that at all,' her mother said intensely. 'He was different in those days. You'd never credit the difference.'

'So you tell me. But I can't remember him like that. The only father I know is a tight-fisted, mean-hearted old rotter who can't live decent for gamblin' everything away.'

'Oh, Eva, Eva.'

'I'm sorry,' she said; 'but it just makes me boil.'

'Look,' her mother said. 'Just look in that album on the table and you'll see your father as he was.'

Eva moved to the table and opened the cover of the album. 'I don't remember seeing this before.'

'I might have shown it to you when you were little. I

haven't had it out meself for years. It was that old-time dance music on the wireless that made me remember it. It started me thinkin' back . . .'

Eva pulled out a chair and sat down at the table. 'He wasn't bad-looking as a young man . . .'

'A little wiry dandy of a man, he was,' Mrs Scurridge said. 'Honest, hardworking, full of fun. I was twenty-two when I met him and I'd hardly spoken to a man except to pass the time of day. I'd never been out to work because your grandfather wanted me at home to look after the house. It was stifling in your grandfather's house because there wasn't any joy or life. It was all God. God, God, God, from morning till night. Not a God of joy and love, but your grandfather's God. A God of commandments. Thou shalt not. Your grandfather was a man with God in his mouth and ice in his heart. I once heard somebody say that about him and I never forgot it. He had a saying for every occasion. "Gamblers never win," was one I keep remembering now. "They might seem to do," he used to say, "but be sure their sin will find them in the end." A stiff, unbending man, he was. I never in my life saw him soften at anything.

'The only time your father came to call on me your grandfather turned him off the step because he wasn't suitable. He came from a poor family and his father had been in prison for assaulting his employer. If there was anything your grandfather couldn't abide it was a workman who answered back. He had half a dozen of his own and he ruled them with a rod of iron. Jobs weren't so easily come by in those days, so they didn't dare to complain. I took to meeting your father in secret whenever I could slip out of the house. It was the happiest time of my whole life. He brought sunshine and laughter into my life and I'd have gone to the ends of the earth with him . . .

'We were married in a registry office when we knew you were on the way. Your grandfather had done with me by that time. We were never married at all in his eyes – just living in sin because of the sin that brought you into the world. We didn't mind, though. We were very happy for a while . . .'

'But what changed him?' Eva asked. 'What made him like he is now?'

'All kinds of things help to change a man. Bad luck, weakness of character. When your grandfather had the stroke that finished him your father was out of work. We were struggling to make ends meet. All your grandfather's money went to the chapel and various other worthy causes. We didn't get a penny. He went to his grave without forgiving me and your father never forgave him. He grew bitter. They were bitter years for a lot of people. He saw nothing in front of him but a life of slaving in the pits and nothing at the end of that but broken health or p'raps a quick end underground. So he began to crave for easy money. He wanted to get rich quick without working for it. It was like a demon that got into him, ruling his life. Nothing else mattered. Everything else could go to the wall. Now it's too late. He'll never change again now. But I made my vows, Eva. I said for better or for worse and you can't believe in principles when it's easy and forget 'em when it's hard. I chose my life and I can't run away from it now . . .'

Suddenly overcome, Eva fell down beside her mother's chair, grasping her roughened hand and pressing it to her own face in the rush of emotion that swept over her.

'Oh, Mother, Mother; come away with me. Come away tonight. Leave it all an' have done with it.

I'll make it right with Eric. He's a good man; he'll understand.'

Mrs Scurridge gently withdrew her hand and touched her daughter's head. 'No, love. I thank you for what you've said; but my place is with your father as long as he needs me.'

Carried along in the crowds that swarmed from the greyhound stadium, but alone, was Scurridge, richer tonight by six pounds. But it gave him little joy. He knew that next week or the week after he would lose it again and probably more as well. His ultimate aim was not centred here; these small prizes were of only momentary satisfaction to him and it was only the constant urgings of the demon, the irresistible pull of something for nothing, which brought him here week after week. He turned right at the opening of the lane and walked along the pavement with his slouch-shouldered gait, chin sunk into the collar of his overcoat, hands deep in pockets, a dead cigarette butt between his lips. His pale eyes were brimming with tears, his thin features pinched and drawn in the biting wind which scoured the streets, turning the slush on the pavements and in the gutters to ice. He still dressed as he had in the lean thirties, in shabby overcoat and dirty tweed cap, with a silk muffler knotted round his neck to hide his lack of collar and tie. The new prosperity had left no mark on Scurridge.

He was making for the Railway Tavern, one of his customary Saturday-night haunts, and as he neared the pub he heard himself hailed with joviality and beery good-cheer by two men approaching from the opposite direction.

'Fred! Ey, Fred!'

He stopped, recognising the men. He nodded curtly as they drew near. 'How do, Charlie. Do, Willy.'

They were better dressed than Scurridge though they were, like him, colliers – coal-face workers: the men who earned the big money, the élite of the pit. The one called Charlie, the taller of the two, came to a halt with his arm thrown across the shoulders of his companion.

'Here's old Fred, Willy,' he said. 'Ye know old Fred, don't you, Willy?'

Willy said Aye, he knew Fred.

'I should bloody well an' think you do,' Charlie said. 'Everybody knows Fred. The life an' soul of the party, Fred is. Here every Sat'day night; an' every other night in t'week he's at some other pub. Except when he's at t'Dogs. When he in't in a pub he's at t'Dogs, an' when he in't at t'Dogs he's in a pub. An' when he in't at either, Willy – where d'you think he is then, eh?'

Willy said he didn't know.

'He's down t'bloody pit wi' t'rest on us!' Charlie said.

Wheezy laughter doubled Charlie up, the weight of his arm bearing Willy down with him. Willy extricated himself and carefully straightened his hat. Scurridge, at this moment, made as if to enter the pub, but Charlie, recovering abruptly, reached out and took his arm.

'Know what's wrong wi' Fred, Willy?' he said, throwing his free arm back across Willy's shoulders. 'Well, I'll tell you. He's got a secret sorrer, Fred has. That's what he's got – a secret sorrer. An' d'you know what his secret sorrer is, Willy?'

Willy said no.

'No, ye don't,' Charlie said triumphantly. 'An' no

bugger else does neither. He keeps it to hisself, like he keeps everythin' else.'

Feeling he was being got at, and not liking it, Scurridge tried to free his arm; but Charlie held on with all the persistence of the uninhibitedly drunk.

'Oh, come on now, don't be like that, Fred. I'm on'y havin' a bit o' fun. I allus thought you'd a sense o' yumour. I like a feller with a sense o' yumour.'

'Come on inside,' Scurridge said. 'Come on an' have a pint.'

'Now yer talkin', Fred lad,' Charlie said. 'Now yer bloody well an' talkin'!'

They followed Scurridge up the stone steps and into the passage, where he would have gone into the taproom but for the pressure of Charlie's hand on his back. 'In 'ere's best,' Charlie said. 'Let's go where there's a bit o' bloody life.' He pushed open the door of the concert room. Beyond the fug of tobacco smoke there could be seen a comedian on the low stage, a plump young man in a tight brown suit and red tie. He was telling the audience of the time he had taken his girl friend to London and some laughter broke from the people seated there as he reached the risqué punchline of the story. 'Over there,' Charlie said, pushing Scurridge and Willy towards an empty table. As they sat down the waiter turned from serving a party nearby and Charlie looked expectantly at Scurridge.

'What yer drinkin'?' Scurridge said.

'Bitter,' Charlie said.

'Bitter,' Willy said.

Scurridge nodded. 'Bitter.'

'Pints?' the waiter said.

'Pints,' Charlie said.

The waiter went away and Charlie said, 'Had any luck tonight, Fred?'

'I can't grumble,' Scurridge said.

Charlie gave Willy a nudge. 'Hear that, Willy? He might ha' won fifty quid tonight, but he's not sayin' owt. He tells you what he wants you to know, Fred does, an' no more.'

'He does right,' Willy said.

'O' course he does, Willy. I'm not *bla*min' him. Us colliers, we all talk too much, tell everybody us business. Everybody knows how much we earn. They can all weigh us up. But they can't weigh Fred up. He keeps his mouth shut. He's the sort o' feller 'at puts a little cross on his football pools coupon – y'know, no publicity if you win. Wha, he might be a bloody millionaire already, for all we know, Willy.'

'Talk some sense,' Scurridge said. 'Think I'd be sweatin' me guts out every day like I am if I'd enough brass to chuck it?'

'I don't know, Fred. Some fellers I've heard tell of keep on workin' as a hobby-like.'

'A fine bloody hobby.'

The waiter put the drinks on the table and Scurridge paid him. Charlie lifted his glass and drank deeply, saying first, 'Your continued good 'ealth, Fred me lad.'

Scurridge and Willy drank in silence.

'Well,' said Charlie, putting the half-empty glass back on the table and wiping his lips with the back of his hand, 'Is'll be able to tell me mates summat now.'

'Tell 'em what?' Scurridge asked.

' 'At I've had a pint wi' Fred Scurridge. They'll never bloody believe me.'

This continued reference to his supposed meanness

angered Scurridge and he flushed. 'You've got yer bloody ale, haven't yer?' he said. 'Well you'd better sup it an' enjoy it, 'cos you won't get any more off me.'

'I know that, Fred,' said Charlie, in great good humour, 'an' I am enjoying it. I can't remember when I enjoyed a pint as much.'

Scurridge turned his head and looked sulkily round the room. The entertainer had come to the end of his patter and now, accompanied by an elderly man on the upright piano, was singing a ballad in a hard, unmusical, pseudo-Irish tenor voice. Scurridge scowled in distaste. The noise irritated him. He hated music in pubs, preferring a quiet atmosphere of darts and male conversation as a background to his drinking. He lifted his glass, looking over its rim at Charlie who was slumped against Willy now, relating some anecdote of the morning's work. Scurridge emptied the glass and Charlie looked up as he scraped back his chair.

'Not goin', are yer, Fred? Aren't you havin' one wi' me?'

'I'm off next door where it's quiet,' Scurridge said.

'Well, just as yer like, Fred. So long, lad. Be seein' yer!'

Relieved at being free of them so easily, Scurridge went out and across the passage into the taproom. The landlord himself was in attendance there and seeing Scurridge walk through the room to the far end of the bar, he drew a pint of bitter without being asked for it and placed the glass in front of Scurridge. 'Cold out?' Scurridge nodded. 'Perishin'.' He pulled himself up on to a stool, ignoring the men standing near him and the noise coming faintly from the concert room. Close behind him, where he sat, four men he knew, colliers like himself, were gathered

round a table, talking as the dominoes clicked, talking
as all colliers talk, of work . . .

'So when he comes down on t'face, I says, "I reckon
there'll be a bit extra in this weekend for all this watter
we're workin' in?" An' he says, "Watter! Yer don't know
what it is to work in watter!" "An' what do yer think this
is seepin' ovver me clog tops, then," I says: "bloody pale
ale?"'

Scurridge shut his ears to their talk. He never willingly
thought of the pit once he was out of it; and he hated every
moment he spent down there in the dark, toiling like an
animal. That was what you were, an animal, grubbing
your livelihood out of the earth's bowels. He could feel
the years beginning to tell on him now. He was getting to
an age when most men turned their backs on contract
work and took an easier job. But he could not bear to let
the money go. While there was good money to be earned,
he would earn it. Until the day when he could say
good-bye to it all . . .

He drank greedily, in deep swallows, and the level in
his glass lowered rapidly. When he set it down empty the
landlord came along and silently refilled it, again without
needing to be asked. Then with the full glass beside him
Scurridge prepared to check his football pool forecasts.
He put on his spectacles and taking out a copy of the
sports final, laid it on the bar, folded at the results of the
day's matches. Beside the newspaper he put the copy
coupon on which his forecasts were recorded, and with
a stub of pencil in his fingers he began to check his entries.
It was a long and involved procedure, for Scurridge's
forecasts were laid out according to a system evolved by
him over the years. They spread right across the coupon,
occupying many lines, and could only be checked by

constant reference to the master plan, which was recorded on two scraps of paper which he carried in a dirty envelope in an inner pocket. Consequently the glass at his elbow had been quietly refilled again before he came near to the end of his check and a gradual intensification of his concentration began to betray in him the presence of a growing excitement. And then the movements of the pencil ceased altogether and Scurridge became very still. The noises of the taproom seemed to recede, leaving him alone and very quiet, so that he became conscious of his own heart-beats.

Mother and daughter heard at the same time the low growl of the motor-cycle as it approached the house.

'That'll be Eric now,' said Eva, glancing at her wrist-watch. 'He said about ten.' She reached for her boots and slipped her feet into them.

'Won't you have a cup o' tea before you go?'

'No, thanks, love.' Eva stood up. 'We really haven't time tonight. We promised to call an' see some friends,' She reached for her handbag and felt inside it. 'Before I forget . . . Here, take this.' She held out her hand, palm down. 'It'll come in handy.'

Her mother had automatically put out her own hand before she realised that it was a ten shilling note she was being offered. 'No,' she said. 'Thanks all the same; but it isn't your place to give me money.'

'I can give you a present, can't I?' Eva said. 'Take it an' treat yourself to something nice. You don't get many treats.'

'How should I explain it to your father?' Mrs Scurridge said. 'He thinks I squander his money as it is. And I couldn't tell him you'd given it to me.'

Eva put the note back in her bag. 'All right. If that's the way you feel about it . . .'

'I don't want you to be offended about it,' her mother said. 'But you know how it is.'

'Yes,' Eva said, 'I know how it is.'

The sound of the motor-cycle had died now at the back of the house and there was a knock on the door. Eva went out into the passage and returned with Eric, her husband. He said, 'Evenin'' to Mrs Scurridge and stood just inside the doorway, looking sheepishly round the room, then at his wife who had put on her coat and was now adjusting her headscarf over her ears. He was a big fair young man, wearing a heavy leather riding-coat and thigh-length boots. A crash helmet and goggles dangled from one hand.

'It'll be cold riding your bike tonight, I expect?' Mrs Scurridge said. She felt awkward with her son-in-law, for she had had no chance of getting to know him.

His eyes rested on her for a second before flitting back to Eva. 'It's not so bad if you're well wrapped up,' he said. 'Ready, love?' he said to Eva.

'All about.' She picked up her handbag and kissed her mother on the cheek. 'I'll pop over again as soon as I can. An' you'll have to make an' effort to get over to see us.'

'I'll be surprising you one of these days.'

'Well, you know you're welcome any time,' Eva said. 'Isn't she, Eric?'

'Yes, that's right,' Eric said. 'Any time.'

She wondered vaguely what would be their reaction were she to walk in on them unexpectedly one evening; when they had company, for instance. Then she pushed the thought from her mind and followed them out to the back door where she and Eva kissed again. Eva walked across the crisp, hardening snow and got into the sidecar. Mrs Scurridge called good night and watched them coast round the side of the house. She waited till she heard the sudden open-throttled roar of the engine before closing the door and going back into the house.

She sat down and looked into the fire and in a moment a flood of misery and self-pity had swept away the uncertain barrier of her indifference and was overflowing in silent tears on to her sallow cheeks. For the first time in years she allowed herself the luxury of weeping. She wept for many things: for the loneliness of the present and the loneliness of the past; for that all too brief time of happiness, and for a future which held nothing. She wept for what might have been and she wept for what was; and there was no consolation in her tears. She sat there as the evening died and slowly her sorrow turned to a sullen resentment as she thought of Scurridge, away in the town, among the lights and people; Scurridge, struggling through the Saturday-evening crowds to stake her happiness on the futile speed of a dog in its chase after a dummy hare. Leaning forward some time later to stir the fire she was suddenly transfixed by a shocking stab of pain. The poker clattered into the hearth as the pain pierced her like a glowing spear. Then with an effort that made her gasp, and brought sweat to her brow, she broke its thrust and fell back into the chair. Lumbago: a complaint with a funny name, that lent itself to being joked about. But not in the least funny to her. It could strike at any moment, as it had just now, rendering her almost helpless. Sometimes it would pierce her in the night and she would lie there, sweating with the agony of it, until she could rouse Scurridge from his sottish sleep to turn her on to her other side. She looked at the clock on the mantelpiece. It might be an hour or more before Scurridge returned. She longed for the warmth of her bed and with her longing came a fierce desire to thwart Scurridge in some way.

It was then that she first thought of locking him out for the night.

It was a pathetic gesture, she knew; but it was all she could think of: the only way to show resentment and defiance. She foresaw no benefit from it and her imagination, dulled by the pain which hovered across the threshold of every moment, could not stretch even as far as Scurridge's rage in the morning. The immediate horizon of her thoughts contained only the warm bed and the oblivion of sleep. It could neither encompass nor tolerate Scurridge's drunken return and the possibility of a demand for the satisfying of flesh that was a mockery of their first youthful passion.

She boiled a kettle and filled a stone hot-water bottle and hobbled with it upstairs. Then she made some tea and searched the cupboard where she kept the remains of old medicinal prescriptions and bottles of patent remedies accumulated over the years, until she found a round box of sleeping pills once prescribed for her. The label said to take two, and warned against an overdose. She took two, hesitated, then swallowed a third. She wished to be soundly and deeply asleep when Scurridge came home. Standing there with the box in her hand it occurred to her to wonder if there were enough tablets to put her into a sleep from which she would never awaken, and she thrust the box out of sight among the bottles and packets and returned the lot to the cupboard. She poured herself some tea and sipped it before the fire, her hands clasped round the warmth of the mug. At eleven o'clock she raked the ashes down from the fireback and went into the passage and shot the bolts on the back door. Even as she stood there in the act she felt the insidious creep of the old apathy. What did it matter? What good would it do? She turned away and went back into the kitchen where she doused the gas. By the light of a candle she made her careful way upstairs. She undressed and lay shivering between the clammy sheets, moving the hot-water bottle round and round, from one part of her cold body to another, until eventually she became warm, and in a short time after that, fell asleep.

Scurridge stared from the pools coupon to the newspaper. A man came in and stood next to him at the bar counter. He ordered his drink and said to Scurridge, 'A real freezer out tonight, isn't it?' Scurridge made no answer; he was hardly aware that he had been addressed. His mind was a maelstrom of excitement and he put his hand to his forehead and by an effort of will forced himself into sufficient calmness to recheck the column of results. It was right, as he'd thought. No mistake, he'd forecast seven drawn games and he needed only one more to complete the eight required for maximum points. One forecast only remained to be checked and that was a late result printed in blurred type in the stop press column of the newspaper. He peered at it again. It could be a draw or an away win, he thought. If it was an away win he would be one point down and eligible for a second dividend. That one point could mean the difference between a measly few hundred pounds and a fortune.

'Here—can you make this out?'

He thrust the paper at the man who had spoken to him, pointing with his forefinger at the blurred print. 'That last result there. Is it two all or two, three?'

The man put his glass on the counter and took the paper out of Scurridge's hands. He turned it to the light. 'It's not right clear,' he said. 'I dunno. I'd say it's more like two, three. An away win.'

'It can't be,' Scurridge said. 'It's got to be a draw.' He turned to the domino-playing miners. 'Anybody got an *Echo*?' The excitement was plain in his voice and the big miner who passed the newspaper said, 'What's up, Fred? Got a full line?' Scurridge grabbed the paper. 'I dunno yet,' he said. 'I dunno.' He ran his finger down the column to the result in question. It was a draw, completing his eight.

'It's a draw,' Scurridge said. He crushed the paper in his hands and let it fall to the floor.

'Hey up!' the big miner said. 'That's my paper when you've done wi' it.'

'I'll buy you a dozen bloody papers,' Scurridge said. 'I've got eight lovely draws. Eight bloody lovely draws. Look!' He snatched the coupon from the counter and thrust it at the group of miners. 'I've got eight draws an' there's on'y eight on the whole coupon!' The one sitting nearest took the coupon and scanned it. 'See,' Scurridge said, pointing. 'Seven on there an' this one here.'

The collier looked at the coupon in stupefaction. 'By God, but he's up. He's up!'

'Here, let's look,' said another, and the dominoes were laid face down while the coupon passed round the table. 'Lucky sod,' one of the men muttered, and Scurridge took him up with an excited 'What's that? Lucky? I've worked years for this. I've invested hundreds o' pounds in it, an' now it's up.'

'It'll be a lot this week, Fred,' the big miner said. 'There's on'y eight draws altogether so there won't be many to share the brass. Wha, it might be a hundred thousand quid!'

A hush fell over the group at the mention of this astronomical sum from which the interest alone could keep a man in comfort for a lifetime. A hundred thousand pounds! Somehow Scurridge's mind, occupied with the fact that the prize was in his grasp, had not yet put it into actual figures. But now excitement flamed in his face and his eyes grew wild.

'It's bound to be,' he shouted. 'There's nobbut eight draws on the whole coupon, I tell yer!'

He snatched his glass from the bar counter and took a long drink, slamming it down again as he came to a decision. 'I've won six quid on t'dogs tonight,' he said. 'I'll stand drinks all round. C'mon, drink wi' me. Have what yer like – whisky, rum, owt yer've a mind for.'

They passed up their glasses, needing no second invitation, and soon the news spread across the passage to the concert room, bringing people from there to slap Scurridge on the back and drink the beer he was paying for as he stood, flushed and jubilant, pressed up against the bar.

Shortly after closing time he found himself on the street with a full bottle of rum and an empty pocket, in company with Charlie and Willy.

'An' I allus say,' Charlie said, 'I allus say a man shouldn't let his brass come between him an' his pals.'

'What's money?' Scurridge said.

'That's right, Fred. You've hit the bleedin' nail right
on the head. What's money? I'll tell you what it is – it's
a curse on the whole yuman race, a curse . . . An' I wish
I had a cellarful. If I had a cellarful I'd lay in a nine-
gallon barrel of ale an' I'd go down every night an' sup
an' count it. An' I'd let you come an' help me, Fred. I
wouldn't forget you. Oh no, not me. I wouldn't forget me
old pals. What's money worth if it comes between a
feller an' his pals?'

Willy belched stolidly. 'Friendship's the thing.'

'You never spoke a truer word, Willy,' Charlie said. He
threw his arm across Willy's shoulders and leaned on
him. 'Your heart's in the right place, Willy lad.'

They parted company on the corner and as Scurridge
moved away Charlie called after him, 'Don't forget, Is'll
want a ride in that Rolls-Royce.'

Scurridge waved the bottle of rum over his head. 'Any
time. Any time.'

As he passed along Corporation Street on his way
through the town he was suddenly arrested by the thought
that he should send off a telegram to the pools people,
claiming his win. Wasn't that what you did? You sent a
telegram claiming a first dividend and followed it with a
registered letter. But the post office was closed; he could
see its dark face right there across the street from where
he stood. It baffled him for a moment. How could he
send a telegram when the post office was closed? Why
hadn't the pools people thought of that? And then a
dim glow of light by the door of the post office building
reminded him of the telephone and he made his way
unsteadily across the deserted street. Inside the call box
he stared for some time at the black shape of the receiver

before putting out a slow hand and lifting it to his ear. He had never before in his life used a public telephone and when a small voice spoke right into his ear he took sudden fright and slammed the receiver back into its cradle as though it had burned hot in his hand. Not until then, as he stood, breathing heavily, in the call box, did it occur to him that he would need some money. He began to rummage through his pockets. The search produced only two coins – a sixpence and a penny, and he looked at them where they lay in his palm, with mingled relief and regret. Regret that he could not, after all, make sure of his money, and relief that he would now have to put off the complex business of sending the telegram till tomorrow.

Outside on the pavement once more he was struck by the irony of having a hundred thousand pounds yet not having enough in his pocket to pay for a taxi home. He looked about him, getting his bearings; then he turned towards home. On the way he began to think about his wife. Christ! but this would be one in the eye for her. She'd never believed he could do it. No bloody faith. All she wanted was brass for fancy foods and for keeping hens. Hens! God! And still more brass to throw away on that great barracks of a house. Well now she could have brass, all she needed. She'd see that Fred Scurridge didn't bear grudges. She'd see what sort of man he was. And they'd get right away from this God-forsaken district to somewhere where there was life and plenty of sun, and no more dropping down into that dark hole to sweat his guts out for a living. He'd done it now. He was free . . . free . . .

Somewhere along a back street on the outskirts of town he lurched into the doorway of a newsagent's shop, falling against the door and sliding down into a sitting position. He uncorked the bottle of rum and took a deep swallow. He shook his head then and shuddered, making a wry face and breathing out, 'A-agh!' A moment later through the pool of light shed by the street-lamp opposite the doorway there slid the lean shape of a mongrel dog, its rough coat yellow in the dim light. It came into the doorway and pushed its cold muzzle into Scurridge's hand. He began to fondle it under the ears, talking to it as he did so: 'Nah then, old feller, nah then.' And the dog responded by licking his hand. 'Yer shouldn't be out on a night like this,' Scurridge said. 'Yer should be at home, all nice an' cosy an' warm. Haven't yer gorra home, eh, is that it?' He felt for a collar. 'Yer don't belong to nobody, eh? All on yer ownio . . . all on yer own.' The dog sat down close to him, all the while nuzzling his hand. 'I used to have a dog once,' Scurridge said. 'Looked summat like you, he did. A long time since, though. He was a lovely dog . . . grand. He used to come an' meet me from t'pit. He got run over one Sat'day mornin' just as I wa' comin' out. A coal lorry got him. A full 'un. Rotten mess. I couldn't even pick him up an' take him home to bury him. The driver shovelled him up an' took him off somewhere. I don't know where. I wa' that sluffed about it. A real pal to me, that dog was. I called him Tommy. An' eat! That dog wa' t'best eater 'at I ever saw. Scoff a beefsteak while you wa' lookin' at it.' He ran his hand along the dog's spare flanks and over its ribs. 'Long time sin' you had a beefsteak, old lad . . . Aye, well, never mind. Happen yer'll get yer bit o' luck afore long. I've had a bit o' luck tonight, I'll tell yer. Best bit o' luck I ever had. On'y bit . . . never had any afore. Except maybe marryin' my missis. I didn't do bad there. She's not been a bad wife to me. An' now I'm goinna make her rich. Rollin' in it, she'll be. One in the bloody eye for that skinflint father of hers. Left all his brass to the chapel when we were near starvin'. Said I wa' no good an' never would be. Well I wish he was alive to see me now. I hope he's watchin' where ever he is. Never had a good word for man nor beast, that old devil. Not like me. I allus had a soft spot for animals. Like thee. Tha're a grand old lad even if tha are a stray 'at nobody wants. What's it feel like when nobody wants thee? Lousy, I'll bet. Here!' he said suddenly, lifting the dog's jaw on his hand. 'I'll tell thee what – here's thy bit o' luck. Tha can come home wi' me. How'd yer like that, eh? How'd yer like that?'

He put his hand to his forehead and mumbled to himself. It occurred to him that he was not feeling well; not well at all. 'Time we were off home, lad,' he said to the dog. 'Can't stop here all night.' He tried to get to his feet and fell back with a thud that shook the door. He sat there for a minute before making another effort which took him reeling out into the street. 'C'mon, lad,' he said to the dog. 'C'mon, boy.'

He was a long time in coming to the path through the wood, for he walked slowly and unsteadily, staggering about the pavement and making occasional erratic detours on to the crown of the road, and sometimes stopping altogether while he slouched against a wall, the rum bottle tilted to his mouth. The steep path under snow was like narrow frozen rapids – difficult enough to anyone sober, and next to impossible to Scurridge, in his condition. After falling on his hands and knees several times in as many yards he left the path and made his way up the slope through the black, twisted, snow-frothed shapes of the trees, the dog, with infinite patience, following at his heels. Near the top of the slope he caught his foot in a hidden root and sprawled headlong, striking his head heavily on the trunk of a tree before coming to rest face down in the snow. For several minutes consciousness left him; and when it returned he was mumbling to himself and shaking his head in a dazed manner as he got up off the ground and went unsteadily upwards and out of the trees.

He was almost at the back door before he realised that the house was in darkness. He groped for the latch and pushed at the door, thinking at first that it was stuck, and then realising that it was locked. What the hell was she playing at! He knocked, and then, in a spasm of temper, drove the side of his clenched fist at the door panel. 'Hilda!' he shouted. 'Open up an' let me in!' But there was no sound from within and in a few minutes he wandered round to the front door and tried that. As he had expected, that was locked too. It was always locked: they had not used the door in over fifteen years. He came back along the side of the house, swearing softly and thickly to himself. She hadn't locked him out on purpose, had she? *She couldn't have locked him out!* She wouldn't do a thing like that to him. Not tonight, after he'd been so clever. The dog stood some way off and watched him as he stood there in the snow, his head bowed as though in deep thought, wondering what next to do. He felt ill, terribly ill. It was a fit of sickness that hammered in his head and made him sway on his feet. He put a cold, shaking hand to his brow, remaining like that in a coma of illness, during which time his memory seemed to cease functioning. So that when at last he stirred himself again he could not remember what he was doing there alone in the darkness and the snow.

He slumped down on the doorstep, huddling into the corner to get as much protection as possible from the wind, and took out the bottle of rum. He drank deeply, feeling the spirit sear his throat and spread in a warm wave inside him. For a moment it seemed to revive him, and then all at once the sickness came back to him, worse than ever this time, almost engulfing him in a great black wave. He dropped the bottle and put his head in his hands and moaned a little. What was it? He wanted to get in. He had to get in to Hilda. He had something to tell her. Something good. Something she would be pleased to hear. But he couldn't get in. Couldn't get to her to make her happy. And now he couldn't remember what he had to tell her. He only knew that it was something good, because he could recall being happy himself, earlier on, before he came over badly. He couldn't remember ever feeling as bad as this . . . Suddenly he reared to his feet and bawled at the top of his voice, 'Hilda! Hilda! Let me in!' and the dog, startled, ran off into the trees.

There was only silence. Perhaps she'd gone, he thought. Hopped it. She'd said she would, many a time. He'd never believed her, though. He'd never wanted her to go. She was his wife, wasn't she? He'd never wanted any other woman. He couldn't live by himself. Who'd look after him? How would he manage? And if she'd gone he wouldn't be able to tell her. Tell her what? . . . Something good. Something to make her happy . . . He turned and rambled off across the patch of unkempt land that had been the garden and looked with aimless curiosity into the mouldering outhouses with their damp and rotten timbers. The thought came to him that he might shelter there. But it was too cold and he was very ill. He had to get into the house where it was warm. He returned across the snow and looked at the house which stood out plainly in the sharp, clear light shed by the new moon. And after some moments he thought of the window.

He lurched across to the wall of the house and put fumbling hands on the stones. With some difficulty he managed to get one knee on to the sill, his fingers feeling for holds in the interstices of the weathered stonework. He pulled himself up till he was standing upright and felt for a gap across the top of the window. He moved his foot and it slipped away from him across the icy stone of the sill and he lost his balance and fell sideways, his hands clawing at the wall. His right hand described an arc against the wall and the wrist hit the rusted, needle-sharp point of the clothes-line hook jutting out some inches from the stone and his falling weight pulled him on to it, so that for a few seconds he hung there, impaled through the arm. He felt the indescribable agony of the hook as it tore out the front of his wrist and he cried out once, a cry that ended in a choking, sobbing cough, before falling in a huddled heap on the snow, to crouch there, moaning and gibbering senselessly, his good hand clawing feebly at the gaping wound and feeling the warm gush of blood spouting from the severed arteries. And then the pain swamped his already befuddled senses and he rolled slowly sideways and was still.

As he lay there the dog returned to nose, whimpering softly, about him before turning again and loping away to the wood. A few minutes later snow began to fall, swirling down in fat feathery flakes all across the valley and the town and the hillside. It fell soundlessly on the roof of the house, over the room where Mrs Scurridge lay in her drugged sleep, and on Scurridge, melting at first and then slowly, softly, drifting and falling, covering him from sight.

THE DRUM

'I ALLUS reckon you can't judge by appearances,' said Sam Skelmanthorpe, apropos of a casual remark I'd just made about someone we both knew slightly. He pushed his glass across the bar counter. 'Gimme the other half o' that, George lad. Don't know why they ever invented gills. Gone in a couple o' swallows . . .'

'Now you take Fred Blenkinsop,' he said, turning to me again.

'Who's Fred Blenkinsop?'

'Y'know – our librarian. I must ha' mentioned him afore.'

'Oh, yes. The chap who works on the farm.'

'That's him. Now you'd never ha' thought there was any more to him than you could see . . .'

With his replenished glass before him, Sam began to talk about Fred, sketching in his background. They called him Short Fred in Low Netherwood, Sam said, because he stood no more than five-feet-three drawn up to his full height; and if the name came off their lips with dry familiarity it was because he'd lived in the village for the best part of his sixty-odd years and they naturally thought they knew all there was to know about him. But most men have little dreams and secrets locked away in the private corners of their hearts, and Fred was no exception. With him, Sam said, it was an ambition: a small enough ambition at that, but one that had troubled and pestered him for years, sometimes lying dormant for long periods, only to spring into life again without warning, like the itch comes to the born gambler, or the thirst to a man with drinker's throat.

'Aye,' Sam said pensively, 'an ambition.' He took a drink and licked his lips, then looked down at the tobacco pouch I'd slid across as I saw him reach for his pipe as though wondering where it had come from.

'An ambition,' I said, prodding him, but gently. 'It's a curious thing, ambition—'

'Aye,' Sam said. 'He wanted to play the big drum.'

'You mean in the band? But why didn't he, then? Surely all he had to do was—'

'Ask?' said Sam. 'Aye, I suppose so. He'd have *had* to ask. He was librarian an' there was allus some strappin' great lad tackling the drum. He'd have had to ask; an' he couldn't bring hisself to do that because, y'see, in his heart of hearts he thought that wantin' to play the drum was a bit daft – more for a lad than a grown man of his age. So he never did ask.

'A good lad, Fred is; we'd be lost without him. He was librarian when I joined the band, an' he'll be handing out music when I'm under t'sod, I'll bet. On'y one time he ever let us down and that was one night in Cressley Park. Trombones found they had the parts for 'Poet and Peasant,' while t'rest of us were crackin' through Lits's Hungarian Rhapsody.'

Fred had been a miner, Sam told me, but since retiring from the pit he'd done odd jobs for Withers, who kept the farm on Low Road. There was a bench in a garden at the end of High Street – the traditional gathering place of old-age pensioners. But this was not for Fred. And Withers, knowing a good worker, had been only too happy to relieve Fred of the miseries of idleness. And in

addition to his natural zest for work, Fred was of value
to Withers in another way. He was one of the few
men in the district who could handle Samson, Withers's
valuable pedigree Friesian bull. Samson was a vicious
and bad-tempered beast with as much love for the human
race as a boa constrictor. Withers had considered getting
rid of him until Fred came along; and it was with surprise
and relief that he found, after a time, a positive affection
springing up between the little man and the bull. To
see Fred stroking Samson's nose and whispering in his
ear while the great beast stood in something approaching
ecstasy was a sight that, until the novelty wore off,
brought the hands from the fields to stare in wonder.

This then was the uneventful pattern of Fred's life:
the days on the farm, the evenings in the Fox and Ferret
with a glass of ale, and his duties with the band.

'And then one day,' Sam said, 'he got his chance. Day
o' the Sunday-schools' Whit-walk, it was. I remember it
well. Boilin' hot. We were all sittin' round in the band-
room chatting and smoking, and Fred had his head in the
cupboard sortin' the march sheets out. All at once in
comes Thomas Easter, our solo euphonium player. His
face is as red as his tunic, an' he goes straight to Jess
Hodgkins, our conductor.

' "Jess," he says, "we're without drummer. Young Billy
Driver's tum'led off his delivery bike this mornin'. I've
just seen his mother in t'street. It looks like a broken arm,
Jess."

'Well, Jess's conducted our band for nigh on fifty
year an' he's grown used to misfortune, as you might say.
So this bit o' news didn't bowl him over.

' "Well now," he says, when Thomas is catching his
breath. "You'd ha' thought he'd ha' done it yesterday an'

given us time to get another man." An' he sighs. "I don't know," he says. "If it in't a cornet player wi' a split lip, it's a drummer wi' nobbut one arm." He looks at Thomas. "Wes'll have to do wi'out drummer, Thomas, that's all, lad."

' "Nay, Jess," says Thomas, "wes'll sound awful." Thomas, y'see, has played engagements with some good bands in his time, an' he's allus particular about fieldin' a full side.

' "Then some'dy else'll have it to do," says Jess. An' he has a look round the room. He can't spare any of us, an' his eye falls on Short Fred, still busy with the music. He hasn't heard a word of this an' when Jess gives Thomas the wink an' calls him over he comes up as innocent as you please.

' "Tha's been servin' thy apprenticeship in t'music-sortin' department o' this band for forty-five year 'at I can remember, Fred," he says, his face never slippin'. An' Fred, mystified, says, "Aye, Jess?"

' "Well I've been thinkin' 'at it's about time tha made a noise, just to let fowk know tha're still with us," Jess goes on. "An' to make sure everybody hears thee, I'm goin' to give thee t'biggest noise in t'band. Does tha think tha could play t'big drum for us this afternoon?"

'Fred's heart must ha' taken a crotchet rest then. Here's his big chance, straight out of the blue. But not a sign of this shows on his face. "I'll do me best for thee, Jess," he says.'

They rolled the drum from the cupboard, Sam said, and adjusted the straps to suit Fred's short stature. He looked down at the drum, an eager light beginning in his eyes. It was a beautiful instrument, painted in glossy scarlet and gold, with white cords, and the words LOW

NETHERWOOD SILVER BAND inscribed on it in gold letters.

'Tha're sure tha can carry it, Fred?' asked one of the players, in mock anxiety, and Fred said scornfully, 'Carry it? Give us ho'd on it an' I'll show thee!'

So they hoisted the drum into position on Fred's chest and fastened the straps. He had a little difficulty in seeing over it, but there was no doubt of his ability to carry it.

'Just give us a steady beat, lad,' Jess instructed him as they formed up in the lane. 'No fancy work, an' tha'll be all right.'

At a blast from Jess's whistle a few stragglers emerged, fortified for the afternoon, from the Fox and Ferret and filled the gaps in the ranks. Fred moved to his place at the rear of the band and made a few practice swings with the drumsticks. He hitched the drum up higher on his chest and as Jess sounded the whistle for off he wielded the sticks with all the enthusiasm of a schoolboy. This was the life!

One two three – boom boom boom. They were off down the lane.

'We joined the procession at the bottom of the lane in High Street,' Sam said. 'A lovely sight, it was: all the kiddies in their new clothes and the banners. We get to the head of 'em an' wait till they're in order. Then Jess blows his whistle an' we're off up High Street, with all the fowk watching, and the banners flying and us blowin' fit to burst. I allus did like a schoolfeast. And there's Fred havin' the time of his life, hitching the drum up higher an' higher an' leanin' over backwards to balance it, till he can't see in front of him at all an' he has to rely on his view to either side to tell him where he's goin'!

'We were on the way to Withers's big meadow an' it was just on the corner of the lane that it happened. Only the day before the council had dug a deep trench in the road, to check if the water pipes were still there. There's red flags an' lamps all round it. We swung out an' made a detour; but Fred, not seeing a thing in front of him, marches straight on, knocking the tar out of the drum an' generally havin' the time of his life.

'They shouted to warn him, but it was too late. He put one foot into fresh air an', so they say as saw it, sort of pivoted round on his other foot an' fetched up on his back in the bottom of the trench with the drum sittin' on his chest like a great playful dog.'

And he lay there, Sam said, swearing feebly, while the band, unconscious of his plight, marched on and into the meadow. Anxious faces appeared over the rim of the trench and strong arms reached down to haul him to the surface. The drum was unstrapped and Fred examined for injury. Finding that he was only shaken, he sat on the edge of the trench under the laughing eyes of the village folk and waited for his breath and composure to return.

'How much for t'drum, Fred?' somebody called, and Short Fred writhed with discomfiture. They'd be laughing over this in the sewing circles and the pubs for evermore. The devil take the drum! Why he'd let himself in for this he'd never know.

Meanwhile, the procession had entered the meadow. The children, bursting from restraining hands, ran free on the grass, the girls in their pretty frocks, and straw bonnets, the boys in their stiff new suits. The uniforms of the bandsmen were a bright splash of colour against the more sober dress of the rest of the throng, and perhaps it was this that caught the eye of Samson as, disturbed by the noise, he nosed his way out of his unlocked stall and stalked peevishly across the yard.

'They say bulls are colour blind,' said Sam. 'Well, mebbe they are. But they can tell a bright colour from a dull 'un and they can hear noise. An' if it's a bull like Samson that's enough to get its rag out. You can nearly imagine him thinkin' to hisself, "Who do they think they are, these fowk, all dolled up an' makin' their noise in my field? Time they had a lesson." '

Short Fred was, by this time, coming down the lane by the meadow, carrying the heavy drum (he'd curtly rejected all offers of assistance), and wishing himself anywhere else in the world. His thoughts ran on in miserable confusion, the predominant theme being the folly of childish fancies in the old.

'Summat then – some sixth sense – made him turn his head and look up towards the farm. He stopped then as though he'd turned to stone as he saw Samson there, working hisself up to do murder.

' "Heaven help us!" he whispers.

'He sizes up the position at a glance. There's the bull at one end of the field, and a crowd o' fowk – mostly kiddies – at the other. And even if he yells they've to come half-way up the field to reach the gate. He didn't think for a second 'at there being all these fowk 'ud put the bull off. Not Samson!

'Well, Samson stirs and Fred lets out an ear-splitting yell. Then he throws the drum over the hedge and jumps after it, his bruises playing merry hell with him. From where he's standing now the ground slopes away fairly sharp, and he's looking straight across Samson's line of attack.

'Samson launches hisself and charges breakneck down

the field. Fred gives a hasty prayer and stands the drum on its rim and gives it a mighty old push, sending it bumping and rolling down the slope. Has he mistimed it? It is going wide? And just when it seems Samson's gone by, the drum bounces right between his legs and brings him crashing down.'

I looked over my shoulder. The audience had grown during the telling of Sam's dramatic tale and now they were all agog for more, though surely several of them must have known the facts of that day.

'What then, Sam?' asked a thin-faced man on the other side of Sam. 'What happened then?'

Sam, conscious that he had them, took a pull at his beer and nonchalantly pressed down the dottle in his pipe. 'Anybody got a match?' he said, and several boxes were thrust towards him. He fumbled in his waistcoat pocket and found one of his own. He lit up in a leisurely manner, timing their patience to a nicety.

'Well,' he went on, his head in a cloud of smoke, 'Fred dashes across the field afore Samson can get his legs out o' the drum. And then he puts the old charm on him, stroking his nose and whispering sweet nothings in his ear, his heart in his mouth all the time, wondering if Samson'll turn nasty again. And when he thinks Samson's calmed down a bit he cuts a length o' cord off the drum and passes it through the ring in Samson's nose.

'Then he gets him up, ever so easy like, stroking and talking to him all the time. And Samson gives a few snorts and shakes his head a bit, and lets hisself be led up the field. When he's safely shut away, and the stall locked this time, Fred goes into the house with Withers, telling him he's right sorry about what's happened. He can't imagine, he says, what made him act so careless as to leave the stall unlocked. A proper day of it, Fred had had.

' "Nay, there's no need for you to apologise, Fred," Withers tells him. "Cause you weren't to blame, lad." And he pulls his seven-year-old nephew out from behind his chair. "Here's the culprit," he says. "Just confessed to me. He thought it'd be a lark to let Samson out. Well he's had the fright of his life for it anyway."

'Well, Short Fred's the village hero after this. An' now he can play the drum any time he likes, cause when Withers presents a new 'un to the band they feel sort of obliged to offer Fred the job.

'But he's finished with that sort of ambition, and he never wants to see another drum. Old Jess nods when he hears Fred's decision. "Happen tha're right, Fred lad," he says. "Tha're not much of a musician, lad." An' then a twinkle slips into his old blue eyes. "But I reckon," he says, " 'at wes'll never see any musician put this 'ere new drum to a better use than tha put our old 'un!" '

ONE WEDNESDAY AFTERNOON

EXCITEMENT boiled in the woman and overflowed in an almost incoherent torrent of words in which the gate-keeper's puny enquiry bobbed for a second, unheeded, and was lost.

'An accident, y'say?' he asked again as the woman caught at her breath. 'Jack Lister?'

Her vigorous nod set heavy flesh trembling on cheeks and chin. 'His wife . . . I'm his mother. They've taken her to hospital.'

'Just a minute, then.' The gatekeeper went into the gatehouse and the woman watched him through the dusty side-window as he lifted the receiver of the telephone and spoke to someone inside the low sprawl of factory buildings. In a few minutes he came out again. 'He'll be out in a minute,' he said. He eased the peak of his uniform cap, then clasped his hands behind his back and rocked backwards and forwards, almost imperceptibly, on toes and heels as he looked down at the woman.

She said, 'Thank you,' repeating the words absently a moment later. Then suddenly, as though a tap had been turned on inside her, the gush of words started again. The gatekeeper listened placidly until she touched on the nature of the accident, when his face screwed itself into a grimace.

'Ooh, that's nasty,' he said. 'That's nasty.'

At first when the foreman spoke to him the man did not

appear to understand. 'Somebody wanting me?' he said, knitting his eyebrows in perplexity.

'Aye, up at the gate. There's been a bit o' trouble or summat. I should go up an' see what's doin', if I were you.'

The man wiped his hands with slow, puzzled thoroughness on a piece of wool waste, then brushed the dark forelock off his brow. He was near his middle forties, of medium height, and thin, with a dark, gaunt, high-cheekboned face. His short black hair with its forelock helped to give him a curiously old-fashioned appearance, as though, once out of the faded boiler-suit and dark workshirt, his choice of leisure garments would be a stiff wing collar, high-fronted jacket, and narrow trousers with piping down the seams.

'I reckon I'd better, then,' he said in his soft, troubled voice; and laying aside the piece of waste, he made as if to walk away.

'I should take me coat,' the foreman said, and the man stopped. 'An' look – gerrit cleared up, whatever it is, afore you bother comin' back.'

More baffled and puzzled than ever, he said, 'Oh, aye, right, thanks.' He reached for his jacket and cap on the hook behind the machine and with troubled perplexity still creasing his forehead, strode away among the clamour of the shop, passing along the walk through the ordered chaos of machines and the jungle-like growth of compressed-air pipes to the door at the far end.

His mother hurried to meet him as he came out of the building into the yard, pulling on his jacket as he walked.

'It's Sylvia, Jack,' she blurted. 'She's had an accident.'

He stopped and stared at her, seeming to be wrested from his troubled absorption by her words and the sight of her, hatless and with the flowered apron visible under the unbuttoned coat. He gripped her by the upper arm, the flesh soft and yielding under his fingers. 'What's she done?' he said. 'What's happened?'

'They came to tell me, Jack. They've taken her to the infirmary. It's her hair – she's had her hair fast in a machine.'

'Oh! God,' he said.

She ran clumsily alongside him as he started for the gate. 'All that hair, Jack . . . She wouldn't have it cut short an' sensible. An' I bet she never even wore it fastened up like other women. She never should ha' gone out to work again anyway, but she wanted too much brass for lipstick an' donnin' up in fancy clothes . . . Your wage wouldn't do for her. Any decent woman would ha' been content to stop at home an' look after her bairn . . . I told her it wasn't right, an' she knew you didn't like it . . . It's a judgement on her, that's what it is . . . a judgement.'

They were outside the gate now and still her voice went on and on, clamouring at the edge of his mind and driving him deeper into confusion. Until he turned on her suddenly. 'Shurrup! Shurrup! I can't hear meself think.' He stood at the pavement-edge and rubbed his hand across his face. 'God,' he said in a whisper. 'Oh! God.'

'What time did it happen?' he said. 'Will they let me see her, d'you think? Did they say how bad it was?'

'Just after dinnertime, it was,' his mother said. 'They couldn't have above got started again . . . It sounded bad to me.'

He set off down the road to the bus stop. 'I'll go straight away. I'll get there as soon as I can . . . Surely they'll let me see her.'

They had to wait five minutes for a bus. The mother stood by the signpost while her son paced restlessly about by the bill-hoarding behind, his stoutly nailed working boots rasping on the flagstones. When at last the bus came he stepped quickly past her and on to the platform, looking back in vague surprise as she followed him.

'Are you comin' an' all?'

'Course I am.'

They took seats on the lower deck. It was early-closing day in Cressley and the bus was almost empty. There was something that rattled with the vibration of motion and he tried with a part of his mind to locate it. Was it a window, or the back of a seat?

'What about bairn?' he said, as he remembered.

'I took him next door. I had to. He'll be all right. Mrs Wilson'll see to him while we get back.'

He nodded. 'Aye, she's not a bad sort.'

He became conscious as they drew near the town of his greasy overall and that he needed a wash and a shave. As his mother, unable to keep silent, broke into the quiet with her sporadic bursts of talk he fretted quietly about going to the hospital in such a state. And slowly then, after the initial shock, real consciousness of the accident began to fill his mind and he stiffened in his seat, coming rigidly upright beside his mother's stout form and staring straight ahead, the big adam's apple jerking convulsively in the slack skin of his neck as he tried to swallow with a throat gone dry with fear. Until, as they alighted from the bus, everything was lost in an overwhelming panic that his wife would die before he could reach her, and he started towards the hospital with long urgent strides, stopping occasionally to mutter with soft, frantic impatience as his mother climbed the hill breathlessly behind him.

Inside the hospital they had to wait again, but the house surgeon, when he came, was young and very gentle.

'Are you her husband?' The man nodded dumbly, cap in hand. 'And you're her mother?'

The woman said, 'No, her mother an' father are dead. I'm *his* mother. They live with me, y'see.'

The doctor nodded and the man blurted, 'How is she, Doctor?'

'It was a nasty accident,' the doctor said carefully. 'I'm afraid a good deal of her scalp has gone.'

'Will it disfigure her?' the woman asked, her eyes fixed on the doctor's face.

The doctor frowned. 'I shouldn't worry about that,' he said evasively. 'It's really amazing what can be done nowadays.'

The man brought his eyes up from the floor. 'I . . . I'd like to see her if . . .'

'Well, perhaps for a minute, if she's out of the anaesthetic, but no longer.' He left them and returned with a young nurse. 'She's in Victoria Ward. The nurse will take you up.'

When the woman made as if to follow her son, the doctor restrained her. 'Just one now. He won't be long. You can sit down in the waiting-room.'

Going up in the lift he began to feel faint. He had always hated hospitals. He realised the foolishness of his dislike; hospitals were places of healing and mercy. But his aversion was to physical suffering in others and here he felt surrounded, overwhelmed by it. The characteristic smell of the building seemed to grow stronger the farther they were carried from the outside world, and his stomach seemed empty of everything except nausea. At the door of the ward he was handed over to the sister, who led him down the triple row of beds to the screened-off corner, where she said, 'Just a minute,' and left him exposed to the eyes of the occupants of the ward who, to his furtive glances, seemed every one to have an arm or a leg raised and secured in some agonisingly unnatural position.

The sister reappeared. 'She's awake. Now no noise or excitement. I'll come back when your time's up.'

He tiptoed, ponderous in his heavy boots, behind the screen. She was lying there, her lips pale and bloodless, her face a dead, pasty white against the crisp skull-cap of bandages and the pillow under her head. Her eyes flickered open. 'Jack.' He swallowed painfully. 'Aye, it's on'y me, Sylvia. It's on'y Jack.' He pulled forward a chair and sat down, fiddling uneasily with his cap for a time before letting it slip to the floor between his knees.

She watched him, her eyes dull and heavy-lidded. 'It's a mess, Jack, in't it?' she whispered then.

He groped for something to say. 'How did it happen?'

'I don't know really. It was so sudden. I was just reachin' over for somethin' an' all of a sudden me hair was fast round the spindle an' it was pullin' me in . . .' She closed her eyes and her body trembled under the sheets. 'It was awful . . .'

'It's about time they had t'Factory Inspector round that place,' he said in an angry whisper. 'I've heard some tales about 'em.' He looked at her. 'Does it pain you much?'

She moved her head feebly. 'Not now . . . It did at first, but they give me somethin' to stop it a bit.' The beginnings of a bitter little smile touched her lips. 'This is one up for you an' your mother, in't it? It's your turn to crow now.'

'No,' he said urgently. 'No, it's not like that.' He stopped, wringing his hands in helplessness. He wanted to say more but he did not know how. There was so much that he should say to make her understand. The fifteen years difference in their ages had never seemed so great. But words had never come easily to him and now he was bogged down again in inarticulateness: lost, with all the wordless misunderstanding of their marriage between him and her. He made a little movement of his arm. If only he could touch her . . . But the sheets were drawn right up to her throat and his hand with its dirt-ringed nails and grease ingrained in every line was like a sacrilege hovering above their spotlessness.

The sister returned silently. 'You'll have to go now.' He sighed in mingled relief and despair.

The girl in the bed opened her eyes again as he stood up and replaced the chair. He made a last desperate attempt. 'I'll come again, as soon as they'll let me,' he said. 'An' look, don't worry yerself about it, lass. It'll be all right. It won't make no difference. No difference at all.'

'Look after Peter,' she said, and tried to smile. 'So long, Jack.'

There was horror in the sunlight outside, and in the normality of the traffic passing along the main road at the bottom of the hill, and in the people going about their business, not knowing or caring that she lay helpless in that great building with half her scalp torn away. A young girl rode by on a bicycle, her long hair blowing out behind her. A picture came to him then of his wife's

beautiful red-gold hair entwined in the oil-blue steel of
the spindle and he closed his eyes and clutched at the
wall as his senses swooned and the world spun about
him.

His mother took his arm. 'Come on, Jack. You'll be all
right now you're out in t'fresh air.'

She said little going down the hill, but on the bus she
started to talk again. 'She won't be the same again, Jack.
You could tell the doctor didn't like to say. But I knew . . .
This'll cure her vanity. She'll not be wantin' to do much
gallivantin' again . . .'

He only half-heard her, his attention held by a view
across rooftops where a factory chimney poured out
smoke, thick and dark against the sky, like a woman's
hair . . .

'Now'll be your chance to put your foot down,' his
mother was saying. 'You should ha' done it long since.
Now'll be your chance to show her who's boss—'

He put his hands to his face beside her. 'No,' he broke
in. 'No, now's me chance to show her . . .'

'Show her what?' his mother said. 'Show her what,
Jack?'

He dropped his hands and clenched his big-knuckled
fists on his knees. 'Nowt,' he said, and the ferocity and
anguish in that one word made her gape. 'Nowt . . . you
wouldn't understand.'

THE ACTOR

HE was a big man, without surplus flesh, and with an impassivity of face that hid extreme shyness, and which, allied with his striking build, made him look more than anything else, as he walked homewards in the early evening in fawn macintosh and trilby hat, like a plain-clothes policeman going quietly and efficiently about his business, with trouble for someone at the end of it.

All his adult life people had been saying to him, 'You should have been a policeman, Mr Royston,' or, more familiarly, 'You've missed your way, Albert. You're cut out for a copper, lad.' But he would smile in his quiet, patient way, as though no one had ever said it before, and almost always give exactly the same reply: 'Nay, I'm all right. I like my bed at nights.'

In reality he was a shop assistant and could be found, in white smock, on five and a half days of the week behind the counter of the Moorend branch grocery store of Cressley Industrial Co-operative Society, where he was assistant manager. He had been assistant manager for five years and seemed fated to occupy that position for many more years to come before the promotion earmarked for him would become fact. For the manager was a man of settled disposition also, and still comparatively young and fit.

But Albert did not apparently worry. He did not apparently worry about anything; but this again was the deception of his appearance. Quiet he might be, and stolid and settled in his ways; but no one but he had known the agony of shyness that was his wedding day; and no one but he had known the pure terror of the premature birth of his only child, when the dead baby he had longed for with so much secret yearning had almost cost the life of the one person without whom his own life would hardly have seemed possible – Alice, his wife.

So it was the measure of his misleading appearance and his ability to hide his feelings that no one ever guessed the truth, that no one was ever led from the belief that he was a taciturn man of unshakeable placidity. 'You want to take a leaf out of Albert's book,' they would say. 'Take a lesson from him. Never worries, Albert doesn't.'

Thus Albert, at the age of thirty-seven, on the eve of his small adventure.

Amateur drama was a popular pastime in Cressley and varied in standard from rather embarrassing to really quite good. Generally considered to be among the best of the local groups was the C.I.C.S. Players – the drama group of Cressley Industrial Co-operative Society. They restricted their activities to perhaps three productions a year and worked hard to achieve a professional finish. It was about the time of the casting for the Christmas production, per-haps the most important of the year, since at this time each group was shown in direct comparison with all the other bodies who joined together in the week-long Christ-mas Festival of Amateur Drama in the Co-operative Hall, that the rather fierce-looking lady from General Office who was said to be the backbone and mainstay of the C.I.C.S. Players, happened to visit the shop and seeing Albert on her way out as he towered over a dimunitive woman customer, stopped abruptly and, waiting only till he was free, crossed over to him and said, 'Tell me, have you ever acted?'

As it was the oddest thing anyone had ever asked him, Albert simply stared at the woman while a colleague said, 'He's always acting, Albert is. Make a cat laugh, the antics he gets up to.'

'Take no notice of him,' Albert said. 'He's kiddin'.'

'What I mean,' the lady said, 'is, have you had any experience of dramatics?'

'Dramatics?' Albert said.

'Taking part in plays.'

Albert gave a short laugh and shook his head.

'There's a chap coming from M.G.M. to see him next week,' the facetious colleague said. 'Cressley's answer to Alan Ladd.'

Ignoring the irrepressible one, the lady continued her interrogation of Albert with: 'Has anyone ever told you you look like a policeman?'

'I believe it has been mentioned,' said Albert, wondering if the woman had nothing better to do than stand here asking him daft questions all morning.

She now looked Albert over in silence for some moments until, unable to bear her scrutiny for another second, he bent down and pretended to look for something under the counter. He had his head down there when she spoke again and he thought for a moment he had misheard her.

'Eh?' he said, straightening up.

'I said, would you be interested in a part in our new production? You know, the C.I.C.S. Players. We're doing R. Belton Wilkins's *The Son of the House* for the Christmas Festival and there's a part in it for a police constable. We've no one in the group who fits the role nearly so well as you.'

'But *I* can't act,' Albert said. 'I've never done anything like that before.'

'It's only a small part – about a page. You'd soon learn it. And you'd find it great fun to be part of a group effort. There's nothing quite like the thrill of the stage, you know.'

'Aye, happen it's all right if you're that way inclined,' Albert said, and was relieved to see a customer at the lady's elbow.

'Well, I won't keep you from your work,' she said; 'but think it over. We'd love to have you, and you'd never regret it. We start rehearsals next week. I'll pop in and see you again later. Think it over.'

'Aye, aye,' Albert said. 'I'll think it over.' Meaning that he would dismiss it from his mind for the nonsense it was as soon as she was gone. Acting! Him!

But he did not dismiss it from his mind. A part of his mind was occupied with it all morning as he attended to his customers; and at lunch-time, when the door had been locked, he went over to one of the young lady assistants from the opposite counter.

'You're mixed up with this acting thing, aren't you?'

'The Players?' the girl said. 'Oh yes. It's grand fun. We're doing R. Belton Wilkins's latest West End success for our next production.'

'Aye,' Albert said, 'I've been hearin' so. I've had yon' woman on to me this morning.'

'You mean Mrs Bostock. I saw her talking to you. A real tartar, she is. Terrifically keen and efficient. I don't know what we'd do without her.'

'She's been doin' a bit o' recruitin' this morning,' Albert said. 'Been on to me to take a part in this new play. Don't know what she's thinkin' about.' All morning a new feeling had been growing in him and now he realised that he was pleased and flattered by Mrs Bostock's approach, nonsense though it undoubtedly was. 'I always thought you wanted these la-di-da chaps for play-actin',' he said; 'not ord'nary chaps like me.'

'I don't know,' the girl said, unbuttoning her overall. 'What part does she want you for?'

'The policeman.'

'Well, there you are. Perfect type-casting. You look the part exactly.'

'But they'd know straight away 'at I wasn't an actor, soon as I opened me mouth.'

'They don't want to know you're an actor. They want to think you're a policeman.'

'But I can't put it on.'

'Policemen don't put it on, do they? You'd just have to be yourself and you'd be perfect.'

'And I've no head for remembering lines,' Albert said.

'How do you know if you've never tried?'

'Hmm,' Albert said.

'Look,' the girl said, 'I'll bring my copy of the play back after dinner and you can have a look at the part. As far as I remember, it's not very long.'

'Oh, don't bother,' Albert said. 'I'm not thinkin' o' doin' it.'

'No bother,' the girl said. 'You just have a look at it and see.'

That afternoon, in the intervals between attending to customers, Albert could be seen paying great attention to something slightly below the level of the counter; and when the shop had closed for the day he approached the girl who had lent him the book and said, 'Will you be wantin' this tonight? I thought I might take it home an' have a look at it.'

'It's getting you, then?'

'Well, I've read it about half-way through,' Albert said, 'an' I've got interested like. In the story, I mean. I'd like to see how it ends, if you can spare the book.'

'You can borrow it,' the girl said. 'You'll find it very gripping near the end. It ran for over two years in London.'

'You don't say so,' Albert said. 'That's a long time.'

'Of course, we're only doing one performance,' the girl said, 'so you needn't get the wind up.'

'What d'you think happened at the shop today?' Albert asked Alice after tea that evening.

Alice said she couldn't imagine.

'We had that Mrs Bostock down from General Office an' she asked me if I'd like a part in this new play they're getting up.'

'You?' Alice said. 'She asked you?'

'Aye, I knew it,' Albert said. 'I knew you'd think it was daft an' all.'

'I don't think it's daft at all,' Alice said. 'I'm surprised, but I don't think it's daft. What sort of part does she want you to play?'

'Guess,' Albert said. 'She took one look at me an' offered me the part.'

Alice began to laugh. 'Why not? Why ever shouldn't you?'

'Because,' Albert said, 'there's a difference in walkin' the streets lookin' like a bobby an' walkin' on to a stage an' reckonin' to be one. I don't think I could do it, not with maybe hundreds o' people watchin' me.'

'Oh, I don't know. They tell me you forget the audience once you start saying your lines.'

'Aye, an' supposin' you forget your lines? What then?'

'Well, you just have to learn them. And you have rehearsals and what not. I don't suppose it's a long part, is it?'

Albert fingered the book. 'Only a page. I have it here.'

'Oh, ho!' Alice said.

'Well, young Lucy Fryer would bring it for me, an' I started readin' it and got interested. It's a real good play, y'know. They ought to do it on the telly. It ran for two years in London.'

Alice took the book and looked at the title. 'Yes, I've heard of this.'

'It's all about a young feller and his dad's ever so rich and dotes on the lad. Thinks the sun shines out of him; an' all the time this lad's a real nasty piece o' work. A proper nowter.'

'Where's the policeman's part?'

'In the second act. Here, let me show you. This lad an' his brother are havin' a row, see, because he's run some'dy down in his car and not stopped, because he was drunk. An' right in the middle of this I come in an'—'

'*You* come in?' Alice said. 'I thought you weren't interested in the part?'

Albert looked sheepish. 'I haven't said I am,' he said. 'I sort o' tried to imagine meself as I was reading it, that's all.'

'I see,' Alice said.

'Aye, that's all . . . What you lookin' at me for?'

'I'm just looking,' Alice said.

*   *   *

It was two days later that Mrs Bostock came in again.

'Well,' she said with ferocious brightness, 'did you think it over?'

'He's read the play, Mrs Bostock,' Lucy Fryer said, coming over. 'I lent him my copy.'

'Splendid, splendid.'

'Yes, a very entertainin' play indeed,' Albert said. 'But I haven't said owt about playin' that part. I don't think it's owt in my line, y'see. She thinks so, an' my missis; but I'm not sure.'

'Nonsense,' Mrs Bostock said.

'Y'see I'm not the sort o' feller to show meself off in front of a lot o' people.'

'Rubbish,' Mrs Bostock said.

'Oh, it's all right for you lot. You've done it all before. You're used to it.'

'Come to rehearsal Monday evening,' Mrs Bostock commanded.

'Well, I don't know.'

'My house, seven-thirty. I won't take no for an answer till you've seen us all and given it a try. Lucy will tell you the address.' And she was gone.

'A bit forceful, isn't she?' Albert said.

'A tartar,' Lucy said.

'Oh, heck,' Albert said, 'I don't like this at all.'

But secretly now he was beginning to like it enormously.

At seven twenty-five on Monday evening he presented himself, dressed carefully in his best navy blue and shaved for the second time that day, at the front door of Mrs Bostock's home, a large and rather grim-looking Victorian terrace house with big bay windows on a long curving avenue off Halifax Road, and was joined on the step by Lucy Fryer.

Mrs Bostock herself let them in and showed them into a large and shabbily comfortable drawing-room furnished mostly with a varied assortment of easy chairs and settees, and more books than Albert had ever seen at one time outside the public library. He was introduced to a thin, distinguished-looking pipe-smoking man who turned out to be Mr Bostock, and then the members of the drama group began to arrive.

There were only seven speaking parts in the play but several people who would be responsible for backstage production turned up too and soon the room was full of men and women whose common characteristic seemed to be that they all talked at the top of their voices. Albert was bewildered, and then smitten with acute embarrassment when Mrs Bostock, standing on the hearthrug, clapped her hands together and saying, 'Listen, everybody; I'd like you all to meet our new recruit,' directed all eyes to him.

'I'm trying to talk Mr Royston into playing the policeman in *Son of the House* and I want you all to be nice to him because he isn't completely sold on the idea yet.'

'But my dear Effie,' said a stocky young man in a tweed jacket and yellow shirt, 'you're a genius. You really are. Where on earth did you find him?' And Albert stood there feeling very uncomfortable while everybody looked at him as though he were an antique which Mrs Bostock had uncovered in an obscure shop and was now presenting for their admiration.

'Mr Royston is the assistant manager in Moorend Grocery,' Mrs Bostock told them. 'I took one look at him and knew he was our man.'

To Albert's relief attention turned from him and he was able for a time to sit in his corner and watch what went on without being called upon to do or say anything. But not for long. A first group-reading of the play was started upon and Albert followed the action in his copy, amazed at the way the actors let themselves go in their parts, delivering the most embarrassing lines without the least sign of self-consciousness. ' "You know I love you," ' the young man in the yellow shirt said to a pretty dark girl sitting next to Albert. ' "*Do* you love me?" ' she replied. ' "Or is it just that you want to go to bed with me?" ' Albert blushed.

At the entrance of the policeman a silence fell upon the room and Mrs Bostock, still directing operations from the hearthrug, said, 'Now, Mr Royston, this is where you come in.'

Oh, it was terrible. His heart thumped sickeningly. He found his place, put his forefinger under the line, swallowed thickly, and said in a faint voice:

' "Is one of you gentlemen the owner of that car standing outside?" '

'Weak,' Mrs Bostock said. 'Come now, Mr Royston, a little more authority. Can't you imagine the impact of your entrance? . . .'

'Just imagine it, Alice,' Albert said, getting up out of his chair with the book in his hand. 'Here's this rotter of a bloke, who's had one too many an' been drivin' like mad an' hit somebody an' left 'em in the road. He's scared out of his wits an' now he's telling his brother an' pleadin' with him to help him, when the maid comes in and says there's a policeman come—and I walk in.

' "Is one of you gentlemen the owner of that car standing outside?" An' this 'ere young chap nearly passes out with fright, thinkin' they're on to him. And really, y'see, all I'm doin' is pinchin' him for parking without lights. Just imagine it. It's . . . it's one of the dramatic climaxes of the play.'

'It's ever so thrilling, Albert,' Alice said. 'Did you say it like that tonight?'

'What?'

' "Is one of you gentlemen the owner of that car outside?" '

'Well, happen not quite like that. It's not so bad when there's only you listening to me, but it sort o' puts you off with all them la-di-da fellers there. You're scared to death you'll drop an aitch or say a word wrong . . . It'll be easier when I'm a bit more used to it.'

'You're really taking it on, then?'

'Well,' Albert said, scratching his head, 'I don't seem to have much option, somehow. She's a very persuasive woman, that Mrs Bostock. Besides,' he went on, 'it sort of gets you, you know. If you know what I mean.'

Alice smiled. 'I know what you mean. You do it, Albert. You show them.'

Albert looked at her and in a moment a slow grin spread across his face. 'I think I will, Alice,' he said. 'I think I will.'

Once committed, Albert sank himself heart and soul into the perfecting of his part. Attendance at Mrs Bostock's house on Monday evenings opened up a new vista of life to him. It was his first contact with the artistic tempera-ment and he soon realised that very often the amount of temperament varied in inverse ratio to the amount of talent. He was fascinated.

'You've never met anybody like 'em,' he said to Alice

one night. 'They shake hands to feel how long the claws are an' put their arms round one another so's it's easier to slip the knife in.'

'Oh, surely, Albert,' said Alice, a person of sweetness and light, 'they're not as bad as all that.'

'No,' he admitted; 'some of 'em's all right; but there's one or two proper devils.' He shook his head. 'They're certainly not sort o' folk I've been used to. Three-quarters of 'em don't even work for t'Co-op.'

'How is it coming along?' Alice asked.

'Pretty fair. We're tryin' it out on the stage next week, with all the actions an' everything.'

On the night of the dress rehearsal Alice answered a knock on the door to find a policeman on the step.

'Does Albert Royston live here?' a gruff official voice asked.

Alice was startled. 'Well, he does,' she said, 'but he's not in just now.'

She opened the door a little wider and the light fell across the man's face. Her husband stepped towards her, laughing.

'You silly fool, Albert,' Alice said indulgently. 'You gave me a shock.'

Albert was still chuckling as he walked through into the living-room. 'Well, how do I look?'

'You look marvellous,' Alice said. 'But you've never come through the streets like that, have you? You could get into trouble.'

'It's all right,' Albert told her. 'I had me mac on over the uniform and the helmet in a bag. I just had to give you a preview like. An' Mrs Bostock says could you put a little tuck in the tunic: summat they can take out before it goes back. It's a bit on the roomy side.'

'It must have been made for a giant,' Alice said as she fussed about behind him, examining the tunic. 'Ooh, Albert, but isn't it getting exciting! I can't wait for the night.'

'Well, like it or lump it,' Albert said, 'there's only another week now.'

He was at the hall early on the night of the play and made up and dressed in the police constable's uniform by the end of the first act. As the second act began he found himself alone in the dressing-room. He looked into the mirror and squared the helmet on his head. He certainly looked the part all right. It would be a bit of a lark to go out in the street and pinch somebody for speeding or something. He narrowed his eyes, looking fiercely at himself, and spoke his opening line in a gutteral undertone.

Well, this was it. No good looking in the book. If he didn't know the part now he never would. Out there the second act was under way, the players doing their very best, revelling in a hobby they loved, giving entertainment to all those people; and in return the audience was thrilling to every twist and climax of the plot, and not letting one witty phrase, one humorous exchange go by without a laugh. A good audience, Mrs Bostock had said: the sort of audience all actors, professional or amateur, loved: at one with the players, receptive, responsive, appreciative. And soon its eyes would be on him.

He was suddenly seized by an appalling attack of stage fright. His stomach was empty, a hollow void of fear. He put his head in his hands. He couldn't do it. How could he ever have imagined he could? He couldn't face all those people. His mouth was dry and when he tried to bring his lines to memory he found nothing but a blank.

A knock on the door made him look up. He felt panic grip him now. Had he missed his entrance? Had he ruined the performance for everybody by cringing here like a frightened child? The knock was repeated and Mrs Bostock's voice said from outside, 'Are you there, Mr Royston?'

Albert took his script in his hand and opened the door. She smiled brightly up at him. 'Everything all right?' She gave him an appraising look. 'You look wonderful. You're not on for a little while yet but I should come and stand in the wings and get the feel of the action. You look a bit pale about the gills. What's wrong—stage fright?'

'It's all a bit new to me,' Albert said feebly.

'Of course it is. But you know your lines perfectly and once you're out there you'll forget your nervousness. Just remember the audience is on your side.'

They went up the narrow steps to the level of the stage. The voices of the actors became more distinct. He caught the tail-end of a line he recognised. There already? Recurrent fear gripped his stomach.

He looked out on to the brightly lit stage, at the actors moving about, talking, and across to where the girl who was acting as prompter sat with an open script on her knee. 'Shirley hasn't had a thing to do so far,' Mrs Bostock murmured. 'The whole thing's gone like a dream.' She took the script from Albert's hands and found the place for him. 'Here we are. Now you just follow the action in there and relax, take it easy. You'll be on and off so quick you'll hardly know you've left the wings.'

'I'm all right now,' Albert told her.

He realised to his own surprise that he was; and he became increasingly so as the action of the play absorbed him, so that he began to feel himself part of it and no longer a frightened amateur shivering in the wings.

Two pages to go. The younger son was telling his brother about the accident. The row was just beginning and at the very height of it he would make his entrance. He began to feel excited. What was it Mrs Bostock had said? 'From the second you step on you dominate the stage. Your entrance is like a thunder-clap.' By shots! He realised vaguely that Mrs Bostock had left his side, but he didn't care now. He felt a supreme confidence. He was ready. He'd show them. By shots he would!

One page. ' "You've been rotten all your life, Paul," ' the elder brother was saying. ' "I've never cherished any illusions about you, but this, this is more than even I dreamed you were capable of." '

' "I know you hate me, Tom. I've always known it. But if only for father's sake, you must help me now. You know what it will do to him if he finds out. He couldn't stand it in his condition." '

' "You swine. You utter swine . . ." '

The girl who was the maid appeared at his side. She gave him a quick smile. No nerves about her. She'd been on and off the stage all evening, living the part. Albert stared out, fascinated. Not until this moment had he known the true thrill of acting, of submerging one's own personality in that of another.

' "Where are you going?" '

' "I'm going to find that man you knocked down and get him to a hospital. And you're coming with me." '

' "But it's too late, Tom. It was hours ago. Some-one's sure to have found him by now. Perhaps the police . . ." '

Any minute now. They were working up to his entrance. *Like a thunder-clap.* Albert braced his shoulders and touched his helmet. He glanced down at the script and quickly turned a page. He had lost his place. Panic smote him like a blow. They were still talking, though, so he must be all right. And anyway the maid gave him his cue and she was still by his side. Then suddenly she was no longer at his side. She had gone. He fumbled with his script. Surely . . . not so far . . .

He felt Mrs Bostock at his elbow. He turned to her in stupid surprise.

'But,' he said, 'they've . . . they've—'

She nodded. 'Yes. They've skipped three pages. They've missed your part right out.'

He was already at home when Alice returned.

'Whatever happened, Albert?' she said anxiously. 'You weren't ill, were you?'

He told her. 'I went and got changed straight away,' he said, 'and came home.'

'Well, isn't that a shame!'

'Oh, they just got carried away,' Albert said. 'One of 'em lost his place and skipped and the other had to follow him. They did it so quick nobody could do owt about it.' He smiled as he began to take off his shoes. 'Looks as though I'll never know whether I'd've stood up to it or not,' he said.

He never did anything of the kind again.

A long time after he was able to face with equanimity his wife's request, in the presence of acquaintances, that he should tell them about his 'acting career,' and say, 'No, you tell 'em, Alice. You tell it best.' And the genuine smile on his honest face during the recounting of the story of the unspoken lines, which never failed to provoke shouts of laughter, always deceived the listeners. So that never for one moment did they guess just how cruel, how grievous a disappointment it had been to him at the time.

THE FURY

THERE were times when Mrs Fletcher was sure her husband thought more of his rabbits than anything else in the
world: more than meat and drink, more than tobacco and
comfort, more than her – or the other woman. And this
was one of those times, this Saturday morning as she looked
out from the kitchen where she was preparing the dinner
to where she could see Fletcher working absorbedly, cleaning out the hutches, feeding the animals, and grooming his
two favourite Angoras for the afternoon's show in Cressley.

She was a passionate woman who clung single-mindedly
to what was hers, and was prepared to defend her rights
with vigour. While courting Fletcher she had drawn blood
on an erstwhile rival who had threatened to reassert her
claims. Since then she had had worse things to contend
with. Always, it seemed to her, there was something
between her and her rightful possession of Fletcher. At the
moment it was the rabbits. The big shed had been full of
hutches at one time, but now Fletcher concentrated his
attention on a handful of animals in which he had a steady
faith. But there were still too many for Mrs Fletcher, who
resented sharing him with anything or anybody, and the
sight of his absorption now stirred feelings which brought
unnecessary force to bear on the sharp knife with which
she sliced potatoes for the pan.

'Got a special class for Angoras today,' Fletcher said
later, at the table. He was in a hurry to be off and he
shovelled loaded spoons of jam sponge pudding into his

mouth between the short sentences. 'Might do summat for a change. Time I had a bit o' luck.' He was washed and clean now, his square, ruddily handsome face close-shaven, the railway porter's uniform discarded for his best grey worsted. The carrying-case with the rabbits in it stood by the door.

Mrs Fletcher gave no sign of interest. She said, 'D'you think you'll be back in time for t'pictures?'

Fletcher gulped water. He had a way of drinking which showed his fine teeth. 'Should be,' he answered between swallows. 'Anyway, if you're so keen to go why don't you fix up with Mrs Sykes?'

'I should be able to go out with you, Saturday nights,' Mrs Fletcher said. 'Mrs Sykes has a husband of her own to keep her company.'

'Fat lot o' company he is Saturday night,' Fletcher said dryly. 'Or Sunday, for that matter . . . Anyway, I'll try me best. Can't say fairer than that, can I?'

'Not as long as you get back in time.'

Fletcher pushed back his chair and stood up. 'I don't see why not. It shouldn't be a long job today. It isn't a big show. I should be back by half-past seven at latest.'

'Well, just see 'at you are,' she said.

She stood by the window and watched him go down the road in the pale sunshine, the carrying-case, slung from one shoulder, prevented from jogging by a careful hand. He cut a handsome, well-set-up figure when he was dressed up, she thought. Often too handsome, too well-set-up for her peace of mind.

By half-past seven she was washed, dressed, and lightly made-up ready for the evening out. But Fletcher had not returned. And when the clock on the mantelshelf chimed eight there was still no sign of him. It was after ten when he came. She was sitting by the fire, the wireless blaring unheard, her knitting needles flashing with silent fury.

'What time d'you call this?' she said, giving him no chance to speak. 'Saturday night an' me sittin' here like a doo-lal while you gallivant up an' down as you please.'

He was obviously uneasy, expecting trouble. 'I'm sorry,' he said. 'I meant to get back. I thought I should, but there were more there than I expected. It took a long time . . .' He avoided her eyes as he went into the passage to hang up his overcoat. 'Didn't win owt, either,' he muttered, half to himself. 'Not a blinkin' sausage.'

'You knew I specially wanted to see that picture, didn't you?' Mrs Fletcher said, her voice rising. 'I've been telling you all week, but that makes no difference, does it? What does your wife matter once you get off with your blasted rabbits, eh?'

As though he had not heard her Fletcher opened the case and lifted out one of the rabbits and held it to him, stroking the long soft fur. 'You just wasn't good enough, was you, eh?' The rabbit blinked its pink eyes in the bright electric light. 'Nivver mind: you're a beauty all t'same.'

His ignoring of her maddened Mrs Fletcher almost more than she could bear. 'I'm talking to you!' she stormed.

'I heard you; an' I said I'm sorry. What more do you want?'

'Oh, you're sorry, and that's the end of it, I suppose. That's all my Saturday night's worth, is it?'

'I couldn't help it,' Fletcher said. 'I said I couldn't help it.' He put the rabbit back in the case and sat down to unlace his shoes. She watched him, eyes glittering, mouth a thin trap of temper.

'Aye, you said so. You said you'd be home at half-past seven an' all, and we've seen what that was worth. How do I know what you've been up to while I've been sitting here by meself?'

He looked quickly up at her, his usual full colour deepening and spreading. 'What're you gettin' at now?'

'You know what I'm getting at.' Her head nodded grimly.

Fletcher threw down his shoes. 'I told you,' he said with throaty anger, ' 'at that's all over. It's been finished with a long time. Why can't you let it rest, 'stead o' keep harping on about it?'

He stood up, and taking the carrying-case, walked out in his slippers to the shed, leaving her to talk to the empty room. He always got away from her like that. She grabbed the poker and stabbed savagely at the fire.

On Sunday morning she was shaking a mat in the yard when her next-door neighbour spoke to her over the fence.

'Did you get to the Palace this week, then, Mrs Fletcher?' Mrs Sykes asked her. 'Oh, but you did miss a treat. All about the early Christians and the cloak 'at Jesus wore on the Cross. Lovely, it was, and ever so sad.'

'I wanted to see it,' Mrs Fletcher said, 'but Jim didn't get back from Cressley till late. His rabbits y'know.' She felt a strong desire to abuse him in her talk, but pride held her tongue. It was bad enough his being as he was without the shame of everyone's knowing it.

'Oh, aye, they had a show, didn't they?' Mrs Sykes said. 'Aye, I saw him in the bus station afterwards. He was talking to a woman I took to be your sister.'

Mrs Fletcher shot the other woman a look. What was she up to? She knew very well that her sister had lived

down south these last twelve months. Her cheeks flamed
suddenly and she turned her back on her neighbour and
went into the house.

Fletcher was lounging, unshaven and in shirt sleeves,
his feet propped up on the fireplace, reading the Sunday
papers. She went for him as soon as she had put the thick-
ness of the door between them and Mrs Sykes, who still
lingered in the yard.

'You must think I'm stupid!'

'Eh?' Fletcher said, looking up. 'What's up now?'

'What's up? What's up? How can you find the face to
sit there with your feet up and ask me that? You must
think I'm daft altogether; but it's you 'at's daft, if you did
but know it. Did you think you could get away with it?
Did you really think so? You might ha' known somebody
'ud see you. And you had to do it in the bus station at
that – a public place!'

'I don't know what you're talking about,' Fletcher said,
but his eyes gave him away.

'You'll brazen it out to the very end, won't you?' she
said. 'You liar you. "Oh, I've made a mistake," he says.
"I'll never see her again," he says. And what do you do
but go running back to her the minute you think you can
get away with it!'

Fletcher got up, throwing the newspaper to one side. 'I
tell you I don't—' Then he stopped, the bluster draining
out of him. 'All right,' he said quietly. 'If you'll calm down
a minute I'll tell you.'

'You'll tell *me*!' Mrs Fletcher said. 'You'll tell me
nothing any more. It's all lies, lies, lies every time you
open your mouth. Well, I've finished. Bad enough your
rabbits, but I draw the line at fancy women. You promised me faithful you wouldn't see her again. You said it

sitting in that very chair. And what was it worth, eh? Not a row o' buttons. What d'you think I feel like when me own neighbours tell me they've seen you carryin' on?'

'If you wouldn't listen so much to what t'neighbours say an' take notice o' what I have to tell you—' Fletcher began.

'I've done listening to you,' she said. 'Now I'm having my say.'

'Well, you'll say it to yourself, and t'rest o' t'street mebbe, but not to me.' He strode across the room and dragged down his coat. 'I'll go somewhere where I can talk to somebody 'at's not next door to a ravin' lunatic.'

'And stop there when you get there,' she told him. 'Go to her. Tell her I sent you. Tell her I've had enough of you. See if she'll sit at home while you traipse about countryside with a boxful o' mucky vermin.'

He was at the door, pulling on his coat.

'And take your things,' she said. 'Might as well make a clean sweep while you're about it.'

'I'm goin' to our Tom's,' he said. 'I'll send for 'em tomorrow.'

'I'll have 'em ready,' she said.

When the door had closed behind him she stood for a moment, eyes glittering, nostrils dilated, her entire body stiff and quivering with rage. Then suddenly she plucked a vase from the mantelshelf and dashed it to pieces in the hearth. She clenched and unclenched her hands at her sides, her eyes seeking wildly as the fury roared impotently in her.

At half-past ten she was in the kitchen making her supper when she heard the front door open. She went through into the passage and her hands tightened involuntarily about the milk bottle she was holding as she saw Fletcher there.

'Well?' she said. 'Have you come for your things?' Her voice was tight and unnatural and Fletcher took it as a sign of her lingering anger.

He closed the door and stood sheepishly behind it, his eyes avoiding hers. 'I just thought I'd come an' see if you'd calmed down,' he said.

'I thought we'd heard the last of that this morning?' Her eyes were fixed, bright and unmoving, on his face, and Fletcher caught them with his own for an instant and looked away again.

'We were both a bit worked up like,' he said. 'I know how it is when you get mad. You do an' say a lot o' things you don't really mean. Things you regret after.'

There was silence for a second before she said, the same tight, strained note in her voice, 'What things?'

'I mean like me walkin' out,' Fletcher said. 'All it needed was a bit o' quiet talkin' an' it wouldn't ha' come to that. It'd ha' been all right if only you'd listened to me.'

'I never expected you to come back,' she said, and moved almost trance-like, across the room to the fire, still watching him intently, almost disbelievingly, as though she had expected that with his slamming of the door this morning he would walk off the edge of the world, never to be seen again.

He came over to the hearth to stand beside her. He started to put his hand on her shoulder, but as she moved away slightly he dropped his arm again and looked past her into the fire.

'What I said before, I meant,' he said, speaking quietly, earnestly, with the awkwardness of a man not used to expressing the finer feelings. 'I could ha' told you about it last night, only I didn't see any point. It was all forgotten as far as I was concerned. Finished. But she was waiting

for me when I came out o' the show. I told her I didn't
want to see her again. There was never owt much between
us anyway. But I couldn't get rid of her. She hung on like
mad. An' when I looked at her, all painted an' powdered
up, I found meself thinkin' what a great fool I'd been ever
to risk losing all that mattered for a brazen baggage like
her. It took me a couple of hours to get rid of her. She got
proper nasty towards the end. Started shoutin' and
swearin', right in the street. It was awful.' Fletcher sighed
and shook his head and a shudder seemed to run through
Mrs Fletcher. 'I had to jump on a bus in the end and just
leave her standing there. There was nowt else I could do
bar give her a clout or summat . . .'

As he finished talking something seemed to snap inside
Mrs Fletcher and she began to cry softly. He put his arm
round her shoulders, tentatively at first, then, when she
offered no resistance, with pressure, drawing her to him.

'Now, lass. Now then. Cryin' won't do any good. We've
had our little bust-up, an' now it's all over an' done with.'

'Oh, why didn't I listen?' she sobbed. 'None of this
would have happened then.'

He drew her down into an armchair and held her to
him. 'Never mind now, lass. No harm done. Don't cry any
more?'

After a time, he said, 'I'll just nip out an' see to the
rabbits, then we can get off up to bed.'

She held him to her. 'No, leave 'em. Come to bed now.'

He smiled quietly, indulgently. 'Still a bit jealous, eh?
Well, I reckon they'll manage till morning.'

Later still, in the dark secret warmth of the bed, she
clung to him again. 'Did you mean it?' she said. 'When
you said you loved nobody but me?'

'I did,' he said.

'Say it, then,' she said, holding him hard.

'I love you, lass,' he said. 'Nobody but you. It'll be better in future. You'll see.'

She could have cried out then. Better in future! Oh, why hadn't she listened? Why, why, why? If only she had listened and heard him in time! For now this moment was all she had. There could be no future: nothing past the morning when he would go out and find the rabbits slaughtered in their hutches.

THE LIVING AND THE DEAD

He picked his way gingerly between the graves like a man stepping through a pit of snakes. Yet the only serpents he feared to disturb were those from his own distant past, and surely they were fangless after all this time . . .

He found now that memory had played him false. The cemetery had changed. It was bigger, for one thing; the gravestones that, seen from the station entrance on the other side of the river, had seemed to him like litter on a park slope, were set out now almost to the boundary fence, and it occurred to him that soon another field must be purchased. Waste, he thought. He himself believed in cremation, when he thought of death at all. Or, better still, burial at sea: no memorial, no mess.

So he went on, putting his feet carefully into the long wet grasses until he reached the asphalt avenue on the other side; and as he stood there, looking uncertainly about, trying to reorientate himself, the sexton came up the slope, walking with long easy strides, clay-streaked spade over his shoulder. As he drew abreast the man spoke to him.

'I'm looking for William Larkin's grave,' he said. 'He'd be buried ten days or a fortnight ago.'

The sexton swung the spade down and leaned on it, wiping his neck with a dark blue handkerchief.

'New grave?'

'No, family. I thought I could go straight to it, but the place has changed.'

'Larkin . . . aye.' The sexton was an elderly man. He glanced at the other now, but without recognition. 'Aye . . . up here.'

He shouldered the spade again and they strolled up the slope together, exchanging commonplaces about the weather. And when they had gone only twenty yards the man's memory cleared and he found the grave without further direction.

He looked at the marble headstone, resting one foot lightly on the kerbstone until he realised and removed it. It was this same unexpected but unignorable sense of propriety that, a few moments later, arrested his hands as they fumbled for cigarettes and matches. There were two inscriptions on the stone, the upper one more than twenty years old: *In memory of Jane Alice Larkin, dear wife and mother* . . . and below this, newly chiselled into the marble: *and of William Henry Larkin, husband of the above* . . . *a beloved father, greatly missed* . . . 'Greatly missed . . .' That was a good one. He wondered which of them had thought of that. Still, it would never do always to put the truth on a gravestone. Imagine seeing it: *Not before time* or *Glad to see him go* . . .

So they perpetrated the last sham.

He stood there looking at the stone, not seeing the inscriptions now, his mind looking back over fifteen years and more. And so she found him, the woman who hurried down the path between the laurels from the water-tank near the sexton's cottage, brimming flower-holder in hand, red and yellow heads of tulips bobbing at the rim of her shopping-basket. She stopped, seeing him so, and watched him for several minutes unobserved. In his navy-blue raincoat, shabby blue serge suit, and roll-necked blue jumper he carried an unmistakable tang of the sea. He was a tall man, but thin, fined down, the brown skin taut over the high-cheekboned face, with the big fleshy nose and slightly protuberant blue eyes. He had changed since last she saw him, but she knew him for her younger brother.

'Well,' she said, and her voice startled him half-round to face her, 'you came after all!'

Her sudden appearance threw him off-balance for a moment, so that when he spoke it was with a note of gently patronising amusement which was, however, more of a defence than anything else, for there was real affection and pleasure in his slow smile.

'Well,' he said, his voice echoing hers; 'well, well, well – Annie; little Annie.'

'I thought you weren't coming,' she said as she came between the graves towards him. 'We broadcast for you . . .'

'I was at sea,' he said. 'I was surprised. I wondered why you'd bothered.'

'It was Henry's idea.'

'I should have thought I'd be the last person Henry wanted to see.'

'It was Father . . . He wanted to see you.'

'Him – see me!'

She knelt and pressed the flower-holder firmly in place among the marble chips and began to insert the long stems of the tulips.

'There's no need for bitterness, Arthur. We've got past all that . . . Anyway, you've had the last satisfaction of knowing he went without you being here.'

'Bitterness!' he said. 'Satisfaction! He cursed me out of the house . . . stood on the doorstep and told me never to cross his threshold again. You know what happened,

Annie. You were there. Anyway,' he went on when she did not answer him, 'I was at sea. Coming back from Cuba. I couldn't charter an aeroplane.'

'How did you know he was dead? How is it you didn't come straight to the house?'

'A feller down in town told me. I didn't know him, but he remembered me. He told me, so I came straight here.'

He stood with his hands deep in the pockets of his raincoat and watched her arrange the flowers, breaking a stem here and there until they were balanced to her satisfaction.

'You look after it?' he asked. 'Is it your job?'

'It's always been my job,' she said. Then, without malice, 'The others come at Easter: I come all the year round. I've looked after it for Mother all this time and it's no more hardship now there's two of 'em here.'

'There's room for another, isn't there?' he said. 'What about it then? Will you enjoy looking after Henry or Cissie?'

'It might be me,' she said. 'What then?'

'You'll outlive those two.'

'Perhaps,' she said. 'Then it might be Lucy: she's the oldest.'

'Lucy?'

She gave a quick glance up at him. 'Father's second wife, I mean.'

'You mean he married again?'

'Eight years ago.' She got up and looked at him across the grave. 'You wouldn't know about that, never having let anybody know where you were.'

He shrugged, uneasy under her direct gaze. 'Ah, you know how it is. I've been all over the place: Canada,

Australia, Singapore. South America now . . . Besides, why should I make excuses? There's never been anybody I wanted to hear from; or who wanted to hear from me. Except you, Annie. I've often wondered about you.' His gaze fell to her naked, virginal left hand, then lifted again. 'It is nice to see you again, you know, Annie.'

Her eyes on him had softened. 'And you, Arthur,' she said. 'I didn't know what could have become of you. I thought when you didn't come that perhaps you were—'

'Dead?' He laughed. 'Not me, Annie. You know what they say – Only the good die young.'

'And you're not good, is that it?'

Her picking up of his lightly spoken words put him on the defensive again.

'I've never pretended to be better than I am.'

'Like some you could mention, eh?'

'I didn't say it.'

'But you meant it.'

'Look' – he stirred uneasily – 'what is this? First you accuse me of being bitter, and now you put the words into my mouth. I haven't seen you for fifteen years, Annie; let's not be like this.'

'No, you're right.' She picked up the basket and slid it along to her elbow. 'I'm sorry, Arthur. I was just so disappointed when you didn't get here in time.'

'What was it?'

'Bronchitis. The old complaint. Been troubling him for years. The last cold spell finished him.'

They made their way back to the avenue and turned up the slope, walking towards the gate.

'Well,' she said after a silence, 'what did it feel like coming back to the place after all these years?'

'A bit queer . . .' He frowned. 'I couldn't see that it had

changed much – a few estates about – but it was sort of different somehow.'

'That'll be all the years away.'

'Aye, everything seems different when you've been away a time.'

She looked at him with a swift sideways and upwards glance. 'Everything?'

'Well, no,' he said, hesitating, 'perhaps not everything.'

She sighed audibly and his voice when next he spoke had sharpened slightly with irritation. 'We're all the same people, y'know, Annie. Did you think when you saw me of Henry and Cissie killing the fatterd calf? I've been away and they've stayed here—but we're still the same people.'

'*He* wasn't the same.'

'Who?'

'Father . . . You'd never have believed the change in him. You couldn't credit what that woman did for him, not having witnessed it. But I saw it all. I watched it happen, month by month; day by day, even.'

'How did she change him?'

'She softened him, Arthur. Mellowed him. He was a different man when he'd been married to her a few years. All that hard sourness and bitterness seemed to drain steadily out of him. And he wanted to see you again. It was his dearest wish that he might make his peace with you before the end.'

'I was at sea,' he muttered. 'What could I do?'

'But you did come,' she said, 'as soon as you could.'

'Aye, as soon as I could.'

He did not tell her that it had taken him a week after the ship docked to make up his mind, but he felt somehow that she guessed the truth. Anyway, he would have been too late. He felt for and lit now the cigarette he had denied himself earlier and they walked on in silence to the gates.

'You'll be coming—' she began as she made to pass straight out into the street. But he took her arm and restrained her.

'Let's sit down for a minute,' he said. 'Let's talk for a while.'

She allowed him to lead her to a near-by bench where they sat down together, he leaning back, legs crossed, pulling at his cigarette, she sitting straight-backed, hands resting on the handle of the shopping-basket on her knee.

Now it seemed that neither of them had anything to say, and they sat in silence for some minutes until he shivered suddenly and pulled up the collar of his raincoat.

'Cold?'

'It is a bit chilly up here.'

'I thought it was quite warm,' she said. 'A nice spring day.'

'Spring!' he said with a scoffing laugh. 'English weather! Every time I come back from a trip I'm half-frozen.'

'You'll be used to these hotter parts, I reckon?'

'I love the warmth and the sunshine,' he said. 'It can't be too hot for me. Some blokes I know can't stand South America, but I just lap it up. I reckon I'll end up there for good, or some place like it, before I've done.'

She was silent for a moment before she said, 'You've never thought of coming back, I suppose?'

'What,' he said, 'here? What is there here for me?'

'Same as there is anywhere else.'

'Ah, I'm all right as I am for a bit: going places, seeing things. Deck-hand. No responsibility, no trouble. Sign on for wherever suits me.'

'And then?'

'What?' he said.

'When you've been everywhere and seen everything. What then?'

'Well, like I said: South America, or somewhere else far off.'

'It's the same all over, Arthur,' she said. 'There's people and things, just as there is here.'

He threw the end of his cigarette across the path. 'I had all I wanted of this place a long time ago.'

'And you got out.'

'Yes, I got out. And not before time.'

She started to speak again, then stopped and turned her head.

'That's half-past eleven striking,' she said. 'I shall have to be off. It's half-day closing and there's one or two things I must get.'

They stood up and moved out together into the street.

There she said, 'Anyway, there's no need for you to trail round the shops with me, unless you want to. You can go and wait for me at the house. Lucy's out, but you can take my key.'

He shook his head. 'No, Annie. The visit's over. I've seen all I want to see now. I was too late for anything else.'

'But you've only just got here . . . You can't go now. Lucy'd be ever so pleased to see you.'

'Why barge in on her?' he said. 'She doesn't know me. Why bother her now?'

'And there's Henry and Cissie.'

'Ah, dear old Henry and Cissie. How are they these days, by the way?'

'Oh, doing well enough. Henry has his own plumbing business and Cissie's husband's manager of the Co-op grocery. Henry's thinking of standing for the council this time.'

'All nicely settled and going steady. All good sober industrious citizens. No, they've nothing for me, Annie. And I've nothing for them. They've no need ever to know I've been here at all if you don't tell 'em.'

'But, Arthur—'

'No,' he said, 'I mean it. I want you to promise me you won't tell 'em you've seen me. Let 'em think of me as they always have. Don't have 'em trying to reckon me up all over again.'

'Oh,' she said, 'but, Arthur—'

'Promise,' he said, and suddenly smiled. At her puzzled look, he said, 'I'm just thinking of a long time ago. Remember how Father used to make us go to bed early, and I used to slide down the coal-house roof so's I could get out to see that lass over Newlands way?'

'I remember. And I remember the last time you did it, that night in December, with a fall of snow on the ground.'

'And I lost control and shot clean over the edge into the yard and brought Father out to me. You stuck up for me, and Henry spilled the beans.' He looked reflectively past her shoulder. 'He leathered me black and blue, and I leathered Henry. That was the night I finally made up my mind to get out. I told nobody of my plans but you. You didn't give me away then, and you won't now, will you, Annie?'

She looked at him long and steadily. 'I'll never give you away, Arthur,' she said.

'Gentle Annie,' he said, taking her hand. 'Sweet little Annie . . . Why has no man ever married you?'

She coloured faintly. 'I'm all right. What about you?'

'Oh me . . . you know me. Like I said, no ties, no responsibility.'

'And now you're off again?'

'Now,' he said, 'this minute.'

He kissed her lightly on the cheek and released her hand. 'So long, Annie,' he said. 'Take care of yourself.'

She did not move from the spot as he walked away from her. After a few yards he turned and waved, then turned away again. His step suddenly became jaunty, and several more yards brought a shrill whistle to his lips. Why, he could not have said. Not to deceive the passers-by, for why should he want to deceive them? Perhaps to deceive himself, then? Certainly not to deceive her, for the one he had never been able to deceive was the one who stood now and watched him go.

THE SEARCH FOR TOMMY FLYNN

On a December evening just three weeks before Christmas, after an uneasily mild day that had died in a darkening flush of violet twilight, Christie Wilcox came down into Cressley to look for his long-lost pal, Tommy Flynr.

His mates at the factory said Christie was only eleven-pence-ha'penny in the shilling, and had been ever since the war; but like the management, they tolerated him, because he was able-bodied and harmless, and for most of the time as near normal as hardly mattered. For most of the time – except on the occasions when this blinding urge came over him, this unswervable obsession to find Tommy Flynn, the pal he had not seen since the night their ship was blown from under them. And then he would leave the little house on Cressley Common where he lived with his widowed mother and go down into the town to search. Sometimes he would stop someone on the street and ask, 'Have you seen Tommy Flynn?' and the questioned would perhaps mutter something, or just pass by without a word, only a look, leaving Christie standing on the pavement edge, looking after them with helpless stupefied loneliness and dejection on his face and in the droop of his head and shoulders. But mostly he bothered no one, but simply scanned the features of people on the streets and opened the door of every pub he passed, searching the faces in the smoky taprooms and bars. Tommy Flynn had been a great one for pubs.

But he never found him. He never found him because

They wouldn't help him. They all knew where Tommy Flynn was but They wouldn't tell Christie. They just looked at him with blank faces, or nodded and grinned and winked at one another, because They knew where Tommy Flynn was all the time, and They wouldn't tell.

Some of Them had tried to tell him that Tommy Flynn was dead; but Christie knew otherwise. He knew that Tommy was alive and waiting for him to find him. Tommy needed him. The last words he had ever said to him were, 'For Christ's sake get me out of this, Christie!' And Christie had not been able to help. Why, he could not remember. But now he could help. Now he could help Tommy, if only he could find him.

He had walked the mile and a half from his home, letting the lighted buses career past him down the long winding road; and on the edge of town he began to look inside the pubs he passed, sometimes startling the people there by the sudden intensity of his face, all cheek-bones and jaw and dark burning eyes, as it appeared briefly in the doorway, then vanished again. And when, after more than two hours, he came to the centre of town, he was, as usual, no further in his search. He stood on a street corner and watched the faces of the people passing by. He even stood lost in contemplation of the suited dummies in the lighted window of a tailor's shop, as though he hoped that one of them might suddenly move and reveal itself as his lost pal. And all the while the yearning, the terrible yearning despair in him grew into an agony, and he muttered hopelessly, over and over again, 'Tommy, oh, Tommy, I can't find you, Tommy.'

He wandered along a line of people queueing outside a cinema for the last show, looking at every face, his own face burning so oddly that it provoked giggles from one of a pair of girls standing there; and a policeman standing a little way along looked his way, as though expecting that Christie might at any moment whip off his cap and break into an illegal song and dance.

They laughed. They laughed because he could not find Tommy Flynn. Everybody against him: no one to help. Oh! if only he could find just one who would help him. He stopped and gazed at, without seeing, the 'stills' in the case on the wall by the cinema entrance, then turned away.

Some time later the dim glow of light from a doorway along an alley took his attention. It occurred to him that this was a pub he had never been in before. A new place to search. He went down the alley, pushed open the door, and stepped along a short corridor, past the door marked 'Ladies,' and into the single low-ceilinged L-shaped room of the pub. It was quiet, with only a very few people drinking there. Two men stood drinking from pint glasses and talking quietly. The landlord had stepped out for a moment and there was no one behind the bar. One of the two men knew Christie and greeted him.

'Now then, Christie lad.'

And almost at once he saw that Christie was not himself.

'Have you seen Tommy Flynn?' Christie asked him.

'Can't say as I have, lad,' the man said, and his right eyelid fluttered in a wink at his companion, who now turned and looked at Christie also.

'Tommy Flynn?' the second man said. 'Name sounds familiar.'

'You don't know him,' the first man said. 'He's a pal of Christie's. Isn't he, Christie?'

'A pal,' Christie said.

'Well, he hasn't been in here tonight. Has he, Walt?'

'That's right. We haven't seen him.'

'How long is it since you've seen him, Christie?'

'A long time,' Christie mumbled. 'A long time ago.'

'Well, I'll tell you what,' the man said: 'you go on home, and we'll keep an eye open for Tommy Flynn. And if we see him we'll tell him you were looking for him. How's that?'

'What about a drink afore you go?' the man called Walt said good-naturedly.

'He doesn't drink, Walt,' the first man said.

'Don't you smoke, either?' Walt asked.

Christie shook his head. He was beginning to feel confused and he looked from one to the other of them.

'But I'll bet you're a devil with the women.'

The first man laid a hand on his companion's arm. 'Easy, Walt.'

'Oh, I'm on'y kiddin',' Walt said. 'He doesn't mind, do you, lad? Take a bit o' kid, can't you, eh?'

But the film of incomprehension had come down over Christie's eyes and he just stood and looked at each of them in turn.

'I've got to go now,' he said in a moment.

'Aye, that's right, Christie lad. Off you go home; an' if we see Tommy Flynn we'll tell him. Won't we, Walt?'

'Course we will,' Walt said.

Christie had turned away from them before he remembered about the money, and he wondered if he should tell them so that they could tell Tommy Flynn. Tommy had always been so short of money. He put his hand into his pocket and took out some of the notes. Then, at once, he changed his mind and went out without saying anything.

The two men had already turned back to their glasses and only one person in the bar saw the money in Christie's hand: a middle-aged tart with greying hair dyed a copper red, a thin, heavily powdered face and pendant ear-rings, sitting at a corner table with a tall West Indian, his lean handsome features the colour of milk chocolate, wearing a powder-blue felt hat with the brim turned up all round. As Christie went out she got up, saying something about powdering her nose, and left the bar.

Outside in the alley Christie walked away from the pub, then stopped after a few paces, to stand indecisively on the cobbles. Always he came to this same point, the dead end, when there was no sign of Tommy Flynn, and nowhere else to look. He bowed his head and furrowed his brow in thought as his mind wrestled heavily with the problem.

Light sliced across the alley as the door of the pub opened, then banged shut again. The woman paused on the step, looking both ways, before stepping down and clicking across the cobbles to Christie.

He took no notice of her till she spoke at his side.

'Did you say you were looking for somebody?'

And then Christie's head jerked up and his eyes, level with the woman's, blazed.

'Tommy Flynn,' he said. 'I'm looking for Tommy Flynn. Have you seen Tommy Flynn?' he asked with breathless eagerness in his voice.

'What's he look like?' the woman asked, playing for time.

But Christie only mumbled something she did not catch and then, the light gone from his eyes, 'I'm looking for Tommy Flynn.'

A man entered the alley from the far end and walked

along towards the pub. The woman took one step back
into shadow. When the door of the pub had closed behind
him the woman said:

'I know a Tommy Flynn.'

And Christie came alive again as though a current of
power had been passed through him.

'You do? You know Tommy Flynn? Where is he?
Where's Tommy Flynn?' His hand gripped her arm.

'I think I know where to find him,' the woman said.
'Only . . . you'd have to make it worth my trouble like. I
mean, I've left my friend an' everythin' . . .' She stopped,
realising that Christie was not taking in what she said.
'Money, dear,' she said, with a kind of coarse delicacy.

'Money? I've got money. Lots of money.' He thrust his
hand into his pocket and dragged out a fistful of notes.
'Look – lots of money.'

Startled, the woman covered Christie's hand with her
own and looked quickly right and left along the alley.

'Just keep it in your pocket, dear, for the time being.'

She put her arm through his and turned him towards
the mouth of the alley.

'C'mon, then,' she said. 'Let's go find Tommy Flynn.'

Once across the lighted thoroughfare beyond the alley
the woman led Christie into the gloom of back streets,
hurrying him under the sheer dark walls of mills; and he
followed with mute eagerness, sometimes doing more than
follow as in his excited haste he pulled away so that he was
leading, the woman occasionally having to break into a
trot to keep pace with him.

'Not so fast, dear,' she said several times as Christie
outpaced her. She was breathless. 'Take it easy. We've
plenty of time.'

And all the while she was thinking how to get the money away from Christie. He was simple, there was no doubt about that. But often simple people were stubborn and stupid and untrusting. She would have taken him into a pub on the pretext of waiting for this Tommy Flynn and got him to drink; only she did not want to be remembered afterwards as having been seen with him. So she led him on, her mind working, until they came to a bridge over the dark river. She pulled at his arm then and turned him on to a path leading down to the river bank.

'This way, dear.'

To the right the river ran between the mills and warehouses of the town; and to the left the footpath led under the bridge and beyond, where the river slid over dam stakes and flowed on through open fields. In the darkness under the bridge the woman stopped and made a pretence of looking at a watch.

'It's early yet,' she said. 'Tommy Flynn won't be home yet. Let's wait here a while.'

She kept hold of Christie's arm as she stood with her back to the stonework of the bridge.

'What d'you want Tommy Flynn for?'

'He's my pal,' Christie said, stirring restlessly beside her.

'And haven't you seen him lately?'

'No . . . I can't find him. Nobody'll ever tell me where he is . . . We were on a ship together . . . an' . . .' His voice tailed off. Then he said with a groan, 'I've got to find him. I've got to.'

'We'll find him,' the woman said, 'in a little while.' And she looked at Christie in the darkness under the bridge.

For a moment then she stood away from him and fumbled with her clothes. 'Why don't you an' me have a nice time while we're waiting?' She took him and drew him to her,

pressing his hand down between her warm thighs. 'You
like a nice time, don't you?' she said into his ear.

'What about Tommy?' Christie said. 'Where is he?'

'I know where Tommy is,' the woman said, her free
hand exploring Christie's pocket, where the money was.

'Why aren't we going to him, then?'

'Because he's not at home yet.' The woman kept
patience in her voice. 'I'll tell you when it's time to go.'

The thought had already come to her that he might be
dangerous, and she recalled newspaper reports, which she
read avidly, of women like herself being found strangled
or knifed in lonely places. But there was always an element
of risk in a life such as hers, and Christie seemed to her
harmless enough. There was, too, the feel of all that
money in her fingers, and greed was stronger than any
timidity that might have troubled her. So she played for
time in the only way she knew how.

'Why don't you do something?' she said, moving her
body against his. 'You know what to do, don't you? You
like it, don't you?'

The feel of her thighs moving soft and warm against his
fingers roused momentary excitement in Christie, causing
him to giggle suddenly.

'I know what you want,' he said. 'You want me to—'
and he whispered the obscenity in her ear.

'That's right,' the woman said. 'You like it, don't you?
You've done it before, haven't you?'

'Me an' Tommy,' Christie said. 'We used to go with
women. All over the world. All sorts of women.'

'That's right. You and Tommy.'

'Tommy,' Christie said, and, his excitement with the
woman broken, tore his hand free. 'Tommy,' he said
again, and looked away along the path.

He stepped away from her and her hand, pulling free of his pocket, retained its hold on the notes. She hastily adjusted her clothes as he moved away along the path.

'Wait a minute,' she said. 'It's early yet. It's no good going yet.'

'I'm going now,' Christie said, walking away. 'I'm going to find Tommy.'

Stepping out of the shadow of the bridge into moonlight, he stopped and threw up his arms, uttering a cry. Beside him now, the woman said, 'What's wrong?'

'Tommy,' Christie said, trembling violently. 'Look, look, look.'

And following the wild fling of his arm the woman saw something dark bobbing in the greasy water by the dam stakes.

'Tommy!' Christie shouted, and the woman said, 'Quiet, quiet,' and looked anxiously all about her.

'It's Tommy,' Christie said, and the next instant he was free of her and bounding down the rough grass bank to the water's edge.

'Come back,' the woman said. 'Don't be a fool. Come back.'

'I'm coming, Tommy,' Christie bawled.

For a few seconds the woman hesitated there on the bank, then she turned and fled along the path, away from the bridge, stuffing banknotes into her bag as she went. Behind her she heard the deep splash as Christie plunged into the river, and she quickened her pace to a stumbling run.

Standing in the middle of the room, his shoulders hunched, Christie said, 'I found him, Mam. I found Tommy Flynn, an' he's drowned, all wet an' drowned. I couldn't get to him . . .'

There was something of resignation in his mother's dismay. She looked past him to the police sergeant who had brought him home.

'Where . . .?' she said, in a voice that was little more than a movement of the lips.

'The river.'

'He's dead,' Christie said. 'All wet an' drowned.'

'Well then, Christie lad, don't take on so. He's happy, I'm sure he is.'

But as she spoke Christie began to cry helplessly, collapsing against her. She held him for the second of time it took the sergeant to spring across the room and get his hands under Christie's armpits.

'We'd best get him upstairs,' the mother said, and the sergeant nodded. He swung Christie up like a child into his arms, and Christie wept against his chest as he was carried up the stairs to his bedroom.

The sergeant laid Christie on the bed and stood aside in silence while the widow swiftly stripped her son and set to work on his cold body with a rough towel. There was admiration in the sergeant's eyes by the time the woman had pulled the sheets over Christie and tucked him firmly in. She struck a match then and lit a night-light standing in a saucer of water on the chest of drawers. Christie was weeping softly now.

'He doesn't like the dark,' she explained as she picked up the wet clothes and ushered the sergeant out of the room. 'I think he'll go to sleep now.'

In the living-room once more, the sergeant remembered to take off his helmet, and he mopped his brow at the same time.

'Wet through,' the woman said, feeling her son's clothes. 'Absolutely sodden. Whatever happened?'

'He must have been in the river,' the sergeant said. 'My constable said he'd run up to him, dripping wet, and shouting that this Tommy Flynn was in the water; but when Johnson went with him all he could see was a dead dog. Seems that was what your son had taken for this Tommy Flynn.'

The woman bowed her head and put her hand to her face.

'Anyway, the constable didn't take much more notice of it. He said he'd often seen your son about the town, and he knew . . .' The sergeant stopped and grimaced.

'He knew that Christie wasn't quite right in the head,' the widow said.

'That's about it, Missis.' The sergeant shifted his weight from one foot to the other; then, as though he had only just thought of it, he took out his notebook.

'I know it's upsetting,' he said, 'but I shall have to put in a report. I wondered if you'd give me a bit of information on your son . . .'

'What do you want to know?'

'Well, where this Tommy Flynn comes into it; and what makes your boy go off looking for him.'

'During the war, it was, when he met him,' the widow said, raising her head and looking somewhere past the sergeant. 'He was in the Merchant Navy. He was all right till then: as normal as anybody. This Tommy Flynn was his special pal. He used to write home about him. He hardly mentioned anything else. His letters were full of him. It was all Tommy Flynn had said this, or done that. And what they were going to do after the war. They were going to start a window-cleaning business. Tommy Flynn said there'd be a shortage of window cleaners, and all they needed was a couple of ladders and a cart and they could make money hand over fist. I don't know whether there was anything in it or not . . . Anyway, Christie had it all planned for Tommy Flynn to come and live here. He was an orphan. I didn't mind: he seemed a nice enough lad, and he looked after Christie, showing him the ropes . . .'

'You never met him?' the sergeant asked.

The widow shook her head. 'I never saw him, but Christie thought the world of him. He could hardly remember his father, y'know, and this Tommy was a bit older than him. He sort of took him in hand.

'Then towards the end of the war their ship was hit by one o' them Japanese suicide planes and got on fire. Christie was on a raft by himself for ages and ages. He was near out of his mind by the time they found him, and all he could talk about was Tommy Flynn. They reckoned Tommy must have gone down with the ship; but Christie wouldn't have that. He raved at them and called them liars.'

'But they'd treat him?'

'Oh aye, they treated him. They said he'd never be quite the same again; but of course you can't hardly tell unless he's in one of his do's, and he didn't start with them till he'd been home a while.'

'How often does he have these . . . er – attacks?' the sergeant asked.

'Oh, not often. He's all right for months on end. Anybody 'ud just take him as being a bit slow, y'know. An' he was such a bright lad . . .'

'Why don't you try and get some more advice?' the sergeant suggested. 'Y'know he might do himself some damage one of these times.'

'I did ask the doctor,' the widow said; 'and I mentioned it to Christie – when he was his usual self, I mean. He

F

begged and prayed of me not to let them take him away. He broke down and cried. He said he'd die if they shut him up anywhere . . . It wouldn't be so bad, y'see, if he was one way or the other; then I'd know what to do . . .'

She swallowed and her lips quivered, then stilled again as she compressed them before looking straight at the sergeant.

'You'll look out for him if you see him about, Sergeant, won't you?' she said.

'I'll look out for him,' he assured her, frowning a little. 'But I'd get some more treatment for him, if I were you, Missis.'

'I'll see,' she said. 'I'll have to think about it again now.'

The sergeant picked up his helmet.

'It'll be all right about tonight?' she asked. 'There'll be no trouble?'

'I shouldn't think so. I shall have to report it, o' course; but it'll be all right. He hasn't broken the law.'

Not yet, he thought, and put his hand into his tunic pocket. 'By the way, you'd better have this. It came out of his pocket.' He put the wet notes on the table. 'Four quid.'

He caught the startled look fleetingly in her eyes before she hid it.

'Do you let him have as much money as he likes?' he asked, watching her.

'Well, not as a rule . . . I like him to have a bit in his pocket, though, and then he's all right . . . If anything happens, I mean.'

The sergeant nodded, his eyes remaining on her face a moment longer before he reached for the latch.

'Well, I'll get along.'

The widow seemed to stir from thought. 'Yes, yes . . . all right. And thanks for taking so much trouble.'

'Just doing me job, Missis.' The sergeant bade her good night as he opened the door and stepped out on to the pavement.

When the door had closed behind him the widow looked at the money on the table. She picked up the notes and fingered them, the thoughts tumbling over in her mind, before going to the dresser and taking her purse from the drawer. She examined its contents and then put it away again, closing the drawer, and went quietly upstairs to her room.

She took a chair and stood on it to reach into the cupboard over the built-in wardrobe for the shoe-box in which she kept all her and Christie's savings. She knew almost at once by its lightness that it was empty, but she removed the lid just the same. Her heart hammered and she swayed on the chair. Nearly a hundred pounds had been in the box, and it was gone. All the money they had in the world.

She put the box back in the cupboard and stepped down, replacing the chair by the bed. She put her hand to her brow and thought furiously, pointlessly. Christie was quiet in his room. She went out and stood for a few moments outside his door. Then she went downstairs and felt in every pocket of the wet clothing on the hearth. Nothing. She sank into a chair and put her head in her hands and began to sob silently.

When Christie woke next morning she was at his bedside.

'What did you do with the money you took out of the box, Christie?' she said. 'Where is it?'

'He's drowned,' Christie said. 'Tommy's drowned. All wet and dead.'

She could get no other response from him and in a little while she went away. He showed no sign of wanting to get up and at intervals during the day she returned, hoping he had recovered from the shock of last evening, and asked him, speaking slowly and carefully, as to a child, enunciating the words with urgent clarity, 'The money, Christie, remember? What did you do with the money?'

But he stared at the ceiling with dark haunted eyes and told her nothing.

He never told her anything again. The search for Tommy Flynn was ended; and shortly after she let them come and take him away.

THE LITTLE PALACE

WE both knew at once when the removal van arrived, at ten o'clock, on that Saturday morning because there were no curtains at the windows and it was so big that it shut out almost all the light as it stopped on the damp cobbles outside the house. I said, 'Here they are, Tom,' and got up from my knees beside the tea-chest into which I'd been carefully packing the most fragile of our crockery.

Tom looked down from where, standing on a chair, he was dismantling the cupboards over the sink: the cupboards he had intended leaving behind had the new tenants not turned out to be the sort of people they were. The first thing anyone noticed about Tom, I suppose, was his size. He wore his fair hair cut short and he had blue eyes in a guileless, pug-nosed face. The numerous mishaps, small, thank God, sustained in his work as a coal miner were recorded in the faint blue scars on the backs of his hands: hands that were big and calloused and rough to the touch: hands that could be so unbelievably gentle and tender when touching me.

'I reckon everything else is ready, Janie,' he said now. 'I'll be done here in a jiffy.'

I often wondered when people glanced at us when we were out together what they made of Tom and me. Tom so big and so obviously a man of toil and sweat, and me so *petite*, with looks that Tom thought so pretty and ladylike and I'd always considered insipid; Tom with his voice heavy with the West Riding, and mine from which my mother and the elocution teacher she had sent me to had coaxed all trace of locality in my childhood. I'd heard one of Tom's sisters refer to me as 'The Duchess' when I wasn't supposed to hear, but I'd learned to hold my own with them, and Tom, when I told him about it, said it was a compliment, and if I wasn't proud of it, he was.

I opened the door as one of the men knocked.

'Manage it in one trip easy,' Tom said as the two men stepped over the threshold and looked round with experienced eyes. There wasn't a lot. We had been married only a year, and the house was very small: one room up, one down.

As the men started to carry out the furniture I slipped on a coat and went outside; partly to be out of their way, and partly to watch that they did not mishandle anything as they packed it into the gaping interior of the van. And as I stood out there on the pavement I felt a hidden audience watching from the cover of lace curtains. I knew I had disappointed and antagonised some of our neighbours by not encouraging them to run in and out of my house as they did one another's; and now the more inquisitive would be snatching a last look at what they had merely glimpsed as it came into the house a year ago. Mrs Wilde from the next house below came out on to the step. Her face was unwashed, her hair uncombed. She stood with her arms folded across her grubby pinafore, her bare toes poking out of worn felt slippers. When I thought about it I could not remember ever having seen her in a pair of shoes.

'Well, off you go to leave us, Mrs Green,' she said amiably.

'Yes,' I said, 'off we go, Mrs Wilde.' She had been into the house several times, and there was little strange for her to see.

'Don't seem hardly two minutes sin' ye got here,' she said, relaxing into her favourite stance against the door jamb.

'No, time flies.'

'It does that,' she said. 'It does that! You'll know a bit more about that when you get to my age . . . Aye. Thirty year I've lived in Bridge Street. Sort o' settled down, y'know. Nivver wanted to go nowhere else, somehow. Brought six kids up in this house an' all, little as it is. Course, young fowk nowadays wants summat better. Got bigger ideas na we had in our young days . . . Bought your own place over t'new part o' town, so I hear?'

'Yes, that's right, Mrs Wilde. A semi-detached on Laburnum Rise.'

She nodded. 'Aye, aye. I reckon that'll be more your quarter like than over here. I mean, this is nowt new to yer husband. I've known his fam'ly for years, an' they've allus been collier-fowk. But I knew straightway 'at you were used to summat better. You can tell fowk 'at's had good bringin's up. Leastways, I allus can.'

I made no reply to this. I didn't know what to say. For what Mrs Wilde said was true: I hadn't been used to this kind of neighbourhood until my marriage; but I'd become accustomed by now to at least one small part of it – the house Tom and I called home. The first home we had ever had.

'You certainly made t'best on it, though,' Mrs Wilde was saying. 'I wouldn't ha' recognised t'place if I hadn't lived right next door. A proper little palace you made on it – a proper little palace. That's just what I said to my husband when I first saw inside. Such a shame an' all 'at you've to leave it in one way: after all t'work you put into it. All them lovely decorations. Must break your heart to leave 'em all to some'dy else.' She paused and cocked an inquisitive eye at me. 'Course, anybody fair like 'ud be only too willin' to make it right with you . . . I mean, it's only proper an' decent, in't it?'

I did not respond to her probing, but merely remarked, 'Yes, you can usually come to some agreement.' I did not feel inclined to summon up her rather dubious sympathy by telling her that the new tenants, a cold-faced elderly couple, had refused even to consider the question of compensation. And of course there was nothing to be done about it: we had no legal claim for improvements done to someone else's property. It had made Tom very angry and he had almost quarrelled with the elderly man.

'Perhaps they aren't very well off,' I'd said afterwards. 'Or why should they want a poky little place like this at their age?'

'Oh, you're too soft by half, Janie,' Tom had said. 'You'd let anybody put on you . . . No, it's meanness, that's what it is. I could see it in the way their faces sort o' closed up the minute I mentioned the valuation. You can bet your life they're not short o' brass. They're not sort to spend any 'less they're forced to.' He had stopped speaking then to consider the situation. 'Well, we can take the cupboards an' shelves I put up, I suppose. A bit o' timber allus comes in handy. But we can't take the wallpaper an' paint. They'll have the benefit of that, damn their stingy souls!'

'Yes, it's only right an' proper,' Mrs Wilde said.

We had arranged that I should go with the van and direct the unloading of the furniture, then come back for Tom, who had one or two last jobs to do, when we would go on for lunch with his family. When the loading was finished, then, I gave the driver the address of our new

house and climbed up into the cab, where they made
room for me between them. It was only a ten-minute drive
across town, but it was to me like a journey into another
world: my own world of neat houses along tree-lined back-
waters and the Sunday-afternoon quiet of sheltered
gardens. It was the sort of district that people in books
and plays scoffed at as dull and suburban. But people like
that, I thought, had never lived in a place like Bridge
Street. But though it was my own world, and the thought
of living there again was very pleasant, there was yet no
place in it I could call home: not as I regarded the Little
Palace (as we called the house, after Mrs Wilde) as home.
I thought as the men began to unload at the end of the
short drive, of how that once strange and dirty place had
become almost like a part of me, so that ever since waking
that morning, and before, there had been in me a vague
melancholy at the prospect of leaving it. I had chided
myself for my foolish fancies, but it was almost as though
I felt that the house was a part of our luck, and that in
leaving it we might also leave something of our happiness
within its walls.

For we had been happy there, gloriously happy. And
not much more than a year ago I had not even seen the
house. A little over two years ago there had been nothing
– not even Tom. And what was there in life now without
him? Tom, who had appeared and shattered the cocoon
which my parents' genteel, middle-class way of life had
spun about me and taught me to live as I never had before.
It seemed to me that I had hardly been alive at all until
that strange, disturbing afternoon when I first noticed him
from the office window as, tired and dirty, he crossed the
yard from the pit-hill at the end of the shift . . .

I tipped the two men when they had finished, and then

walked through the house from room to room, seeing how
lost our furniture looked in it, and noting with my
woman's eye all the things that needed to be done. And
then I left the house and walked to the bus stop at the end
of the avenue. It was well past noon now, and the sky,
overcast all morning, had cleared and showed great
patches of blue behind the big pillows of cloud. As we ran
into town by a stream which flowed into the river I looked
out of the bus at the black water and saw the breeze-
ruffled surface shimmer, as though someone threw handfuls
of sunlight on to it from behind the willows which, just
there, seemed to me to crouch like big green shaggy dogs
by the water's edge. But despite the sunlight and the blue
sky there was a sneaking chill in the air and I felt in its
touch the end of the glorious but all-too-short summer.

The sun was shining, the sky blue, the day I had met
Tom. Two days after my first noticing him he came into
the big new building, with its many area control offices, to
see the manager and blundered into the wrong office, and
so into my life. It was like nothing I had ever known before,
that feeling which possessed me from then on; it flushed my
cheeks at the thought of him, brought tremors to my hands
and knees, and filled me with a breathless, delightful
excitement. And from that first brief contact, when I came
into the corridor to show him the door he wanted, grew
Tom's awareness of me. His eyes began to seek me out as
he crossed the yard at the end of the day shift, and soon we
were openly exchanging smiles. Even though we did not
speak to each other again for some time a kind of intimacy
seemed to grow between us through the medium of those
daily smiles; so that one day when I had occasion to leave
the office early, not long after the change of shifts, it

seemed very natural when he came roaring up the yard
behind me on his motor cycle that he should offer me a
lift into town, and that I should at once accept. That was
the day he asked me, with almost painful diffidence, to go
out with him one evening, and the day I became hopelessly lost. Three months later, to his open astonishment, I
accepted his halting proposal of marriage.

And all this was what the Little Palace had come to
mean to me. More, much more, than cleanliness and
shining paint had emerged from the squalor of flaking
plaster and peeling wallpaper that had been the house
when first we took it. A marriage had been made there,
had come through its first vital year; a marriage that had
received little but discouragement because of the differ-
ences between Tom and me. I was too good for him, they
had said. I was throwing myself away on a boy from the
back streets whose rough-shod nature and way of living
would sooner or later break my heart. But they had been
wrong; only the walls of the Little Palace knew how
wrong. Those walls had held our year of hope and happiness; our little failures, and, above all, our success. It was
because of this that I knew I should remember it for the
rest of my life.

I alighted from the bus in the station into a swarm of
shoppers and home-going workers and decided it would
be quicker to walk the rest of the way. I was soon out of
the teeming shopping centre and plunging deep into the
back streets on the old side of town: the district in which
Tom had lived all his life, and which I had not been in
more than twice before meeting him. I walked along the
cobbled river of Gilderdale Road, with its noisome tribu-
taries, each with its twin banks of terraced houses, ceasing
abruptly by the blackened upright sleepers of the railway

fence, and, turning the corner by the little newsagent's, came into Bridge Street. A year of it had not changed my sense of being alien and conspicuous and now, walking along its uneven pavement for what, for all I knew, might be one of the last times in my life, I felt even more acutely self-conscious than usual – as though in every house along the way the occupants had put aside what they were doing to watch me pass – and I was glad when I reached the cover of the entry which broke the terrace and gave on to the communal back-yard behind the houses. As I came through, my heels echoing on the brick paving, I could hear Tom whistling inside the house. He was happy today. He had never reconciled himself to my living here. It had been I who insisted on our taking the house when Tom's mother heard of it, rather than wait in the hope of something better turning up. We could not afford to buy at that time. My father's offer of help would have solved the problem, but only at the expense of Tom's pride; and I had seen the Little Palace as a challenge to me, to be faced boldly, without fear. We had won through, and now it made Tom happy to be able, after only a year, to take me out of it and across the town.

Absorbed in these thoughts, I had walked right into the living-room before I saw what awaited me there. And then I stood and gaped in staggered disbelief. The room was as though emblazoned with warnings of a terrible plague; for on each of the walls, stretching diagonally from ceiling to floor across the pale blue wallpaper, and on each of the doors, Tom had painted a huge scarlet cross. And now, brush in hand, he spoke to me over his shoulder as he heard me come in.

'Janie? Little surprise for you. An' a damn big 'un for them two stingy old codgers when they turn up again.'

I turned without answering and ran out of the room and up the uncarpeted stairs into the bedroom. He had done that room first. I came slowly down again. My heart hurt as though a great hand was kneading it brutally, and I couldn't speak.

'Thought of it yesterday,' Tom said. He was putting on his jacket now and he wore a grin which slowly faded as he saw the expression on my face. 'Well, I mean, damn it, we couldn't let 'em get away with it altogether, could we?'

I shook my head. 'No, Tom.'

'Damn it,' Tom said again, 'it serves 'em right for bein' so flamin' mean!'

He wrapped the paint-brush in a piece of rag and put it in his pocket. 'They can have the paint.' He looked at me. 'C'mon, then, let's be off. Take your last look at this place. You won't be seein' it any more.'

We went out, he closing and locking the door behind us, and walked away together. It was about half-way down the street that, to Tom's confusion and distress, I began to cry.

'What's up, Janie?' He stopped and peered down at me. 'What's wrong, love?'

But I could only shake my head in reply. It was going to be all right. I just knew it was. But I couldn't help but cry.

THE YEARS BETWEEN

At fifty-three, when nostalgia could be borne no longer, Morgan Lightly turned his back on the sheep-farming land of his adoption and returned to Cressley, sick for the sight of his native county, which he had not seen for thirty years, and of the woman who had jilted him all that long time ago. With no more announcement than a brief letter to his brother Thomas, his only surviving relative, with whom he had corresponded spasmodically over the years, he came back.

He came in winter and for several days he curbed the impatience that would have had him rush off at once to find her whom he had loved and lost, and wandered the dark town and the countryside, drinking in the sight and sound and smell of all that which, though changed, still held the savour of his youth. And then, when nearly a week had passed, he decided that if he were not to allow the prosaic reporting of the weekly *Argus* to rob his reappearance of its drama it was time for him to appease his other yearning.

Driving up out of the town he felt as nervous as a boy on his first date and on the crest of the hill he stopped the hired Ford and relit his dead pipe. He sat there for a little while, with the window down, enjoying the tobacco in the keen air. Before him the road fell into the narrow valley of the stream, then twisted upwards to the village which, not much more than a double row of stone-built cottages in his youth, now carried a pale fringe of new corporation houses and several architect-designed bungalows and villas sited in such a way that, through a deep cleft in the hillside, they commanded a view of the town. Above the village was the winter-brown sweep of the moors and beyond, in the west, pale sunlight touched the thin snow on the Pennine tops.

Morgan got out of the car and walked across the road to look back the way he had come, at the town. His town. How often had memory conjured it up thus when he was thousands of miles away! There were changes visible – the twin cooling towers of the power station by the river were strange to him – but the hard core of it was the same. And it satisfied him to note that most of the changes were for the better. 'Muck and brass,' they had said in his youth; 'they go together.' But not everyone accepted that now. Light and space and clean untrammelled lines were what they went in for nowadays. The new estates, covering the playing fields of his youth on the fringes of the town, with their wide streets and well-spaced houses; and the lawns and gardens in the public squares and streets that had known no colours but grey and soot-black. The smoke was still there, fuming from a thousand chimneys, but when you planted grass it came up fresh and green every spring. He liked that. It was good. It was good too to see well-dressed people thronging the streets and the market and to notice the profusion of goods behind the plate-glass windows of the new shops; for he had left the town at a time when men hung about on street corners, their self-respect as worn and shabby as their clothing, idle, eating their hearts out for want of work to keep them occupied and feed and clothe their families decently.

He returned to the car, the feeling of nervousness and apprehension returning to him as he reached the floor of the valley and changed gear for the climb into the village. He turned the green Consul into the steep main street where the windows of the parallel terraces of cottages winked and glinted at each other across the narrow cobbles, and he noticed lace curtains flutter in some of them as the car moved along, taking up almost the entire width of the roadway and darkening the downstairs room of each house in turn. An elderly woman, standing in a doorway with a shawl over her shoulders, stooped and stared with frank curiosity into the car. He stopped and lowered the window.

'I wonder if you can tell me where Mrs Taplow lives – Mrs Sarah Taplow.'

The woman directed him farther up the hill, still gazing intently at him as he thanked her and moved on. He had a feeling of knowing the woman and he wondered if she had recognised him. Down in Cressley he could walk about largely unknown, but here in the village some of the older people were sure to recall him – and the details of long ago. And standing on the pavement outside Sarah Taplow's house he hoped that no one had stolen his thunder and deprived him of the pleasure of surprising her as he had looked forward to doing. But when she opened the door to his knock and faced him, gaping at him with all the astonishment he could have wished for in her blue eyes, he could only shuffle his feet like a bashful boy and say sheepishly, 'Well, Sarah?'

Without speaking she ran her eyes over him and he felt them take note of every detail of his appearance: his tanned cheeks, his hair – greying fast now and cropped shorter than when he was young – and the good thick tweeds on his heavy, solid frame. And when at last it seemed there could be no doubt left in her mind, her eyes returned to and rested on his face and she said, 'It is you, then, Morgan Lightly?'

Morgan chuckled, but a little uneasily. 'It is indeed, Sarah. I didn't think I'd startle you quite as much as that; but you'd not be expecting me to pop up at your door after all this time, eh?'

'I never thought I'd see you again,' she said. She took a deep breath as if to take control of her startled self, and turned to go into the house. 'You'd better come on inside,' she said. 'No need to fill the neighbours their mouths.'

'You've given me a turn,' she went on as they entered the living-room through the in-door. 'I never thought to see you again,' she said once more. She turned and faced him, standing by the square table which was laid for a solitary diner, and her eyes, still disbelieving, roved ceaselessly over his face.

'You've come back, then,' she said. 'After all this time.' The words were spoken half-aloud and seemed more of a statement to herself than a question addressed to him.

'Thirty years, Sarah,' Morgan said. 'It's been a long time.'

She nodded and echoed him softly. 'A long time . . .'

He noted the changes of that time in her, but saw with approval her smooth, clear complexion, the soft, still-dark hair, the full mature curve of her bosom, and the proud straight line of her back. He knew her: she was Sarah. He felt warmth and hope move in him, as though only now had he reached the end of his journey, and for a moment he forgot his earlier doubt and uncertainty.

She stirred, seeming to come to, and motioned him to one of the armchairs by the fireside. 'Well, sit you down, Morgan. I was just getting my dinner on to the table. You'll join me in a bite, I suppose?'

In this swift transition from astonishment to what seemed like a calm acceptance of his presence it seemed to Morgan that the years fell away almost as though they had never been, and he was relieved. The reopening of their acquaintanceship had been easier than he had expected.

'Don't put yourself out for me, Sarah,' he said. 'I can get lunch at my hotel.'

But it was a token protest, for it had been comparison of hotel meals with his memory of Sarah's cooking that inspired him in his choice of this rather odd hour for visiting her.

'It's no trouble,' she assured him. 'It's all ready.'
She went off into the kitchen and Morgan looked round the little room: at the well-worn but neatly kept furnishings and the open treadle sewing machine against one wall, with a half-finished frock over a chair beside it. They told their own story. His eyes fell on two photographs in stained wood frames on the sideboard and he left his chair to look more closely at them. One of them, a portrait of a thin-faced balding man, he recognised as being of Sarah's dead husband. And the other, a young army officer, remarkably like Sarah, could only be her son. He turned to her, the photograph in his hand, as she came back into the room with cutlery for him.

'Is this your boy, Sarah?'

There seemed to be something of reserve, a barrier, in her glance, then it was lost in pride as she looked at the photograph.

'Aye, that's my boy, John. He's in Malaya with the Army.'

'He's a fine-looking young chap, Sarah. How old is he?'

Again that unfathomable flash of something in her eyes.
'Going on thirty. He's a doctor, y'know. He wanted to be
a doctor and he wanted to travel, so he joined the Army
and got a commission.'

'A doctor, eh?' Morgan replaced the picture, impressed.
'You must be very proud of him.'

'Aye, he's a grand lad and a good son. He wanted to
resign his commission when Mark died but I wouldn't let
him.' She shot him an inquisitive look. 'Have you no
children, then?'

Morgan shook his head. 'No, I've none.'

'But you did marry, I expect?'

'Aye, when I'd got settled a bit, I married.'

He returned to his seat in the armchair and looked into
the fire. Strange, but even after all this time he did not
find it easy to look at her and speak of marriage.

'She was a fine lass, Mary was,' he said at length. 'But
not one of the strongest, you know. The hard times seemed
to take all the strength she had and she didn't live to enjoy
many of the better years.' He looked up at her now. 'And
you lost your man, Sarah.'

She looked away and he sensed in her a similar dis-
comfort to his own. 'I've been a widow this past five years,'
she said briefly, then left him to return to the kitchen,
reappearing in a few moments with two plates of steaming
food.

'Here it is, then. There isn't a lot because you caught
me unawares. Just as well I had the stew as well. It'll
stretch it a bit further.'

'A mite o' your cooking was always worth a deal of anybody else's, Sarah,' Morgan said as he took a seat at the
table. A faint flush coloured Sarah's cheeks and he looked
down at his plate.

They ate in comparative silence. There seemed so much to say and at the same time so much to be wary of speaking of. At length Morgan laid down his knife and fork and sat back. Sarah had already finished for she had given him by far the bigger portion of the pudding and stew. Now she watched him and smiled faintly.

'You haven't lost your fondness for Yorkshire pudding, I see,' she said dryly. 'Nor all your Yorkshire talk, for that matter.'

'Do you know how long it is since I tasted a pudding like that?' he asked her. 'It's half a lifetime, Sarah. I'm still a Yorkshireman, y'know, even if I have been away all that time. I always had an idea I'd come back one day.'

'It seems like no time at all, seeing you sitting there,' said Sarah, watching him as he felt for pipe and tobacco. 'Though I'm sure I never expected to see you again.'

He glanced at her as he fiddled with his pipe, trying vainly to read her thoughts. He became aware that no matter how quickly now the time might seem to both of them to have passed there still was thirty years of unshared experience between them; and those years could not be bridged by the sharing of a meal and a few scraps of conversation.

He felt suddenly slightly ill-at-ease and he pretended to sigh, laying one hand flat on the front of his waistcoat in what, considering the amount of food they had shared, was an exaggerated gesture of repletion.

'It was worth coming home just to taste that meal,' he said. 'You were always the best cook for miles around, even as a lass.'

Her expression darkened without warning. 'And as I remember you always had the smoothest tongue.'

He pressed tobacco into his pipe, frowning, dismayed at

this sudden antagonism. Surely, after all this time, she could forget, if he could?

She brought in the pot and poured tea. 'How long have you come for?'

'For good, Sarah.' He put a match to his pipe. 'I've sold up and come home to stay. Australia's a fine country, but this is my home. I want to settle where I can see the hills and feel the wind and the rain come down off the moors.'

'You didn't talk like that thirty years ago,' she reminded him, and he shook his head.

'No, but times change, and a man changes in some ways.' He looked into her face. 'In some ways he never changes, though.'

She did not hold his look but sipped tea from her cup, looking past him through the lace-curtained window into the narrow street. He wished once again for the power to read her mind.

'So you must have made that fortune you were always talking about?' she said abruptly and Morgan smiled at her bluntness.

'Hardly that, lass,' he said. 'But enough to live on quietly for the rest of me days.'

They talked on in a desultory manner for another hour, until Morgan became aware that she could not work properly with him there. He left her then, promising to call again soon, and he went away still uneasily aware of the undercurrent of antagonism which had showed itself in that one remark of Sarah's. He visited her several times in the next few weeks and took her for drives in the country and once to dinner and a theatre in repayment for her hospitality. But always he was conscious of the barrier of reserve through which he could not seem to break.

At last he could stand it no longer. He was sure now of what he wanted. He had known it before starting for home and it had needed only the sight of her to confirm it. She was still the same lass he had courted all those years ago, and he was still the same chap in his feelings for her. This thrusting and parrying which continued through their every meeting was getting them nowhere. If memories of thirty years ago still rankled they must be brought out into the open and examined and given the importance due to them and no more. And he knew the way to bring that about.

Yet when he came to broach the subject he did not find it easy. After all, he thought, she had preferred someone else before, and why should she feel differently now?

Sitting by her fireside, he made a great show of cleaning his pipe, screwing himself all the while to the point where he could say what he wanted to say. Abruptly, but with a studied casualness, he said, 'I've bought Greystone Cottage, Sarah. You remember the place. We used to fancy it in the old days when old Phillips lived there. Well his son's been occupying it apparently and now he's dead – he wasn't married – and the place was put up for auction. I bought it yesterday . . . gave 'em their price . . .'

He waited for her to say something now that the first direct reference to their past relationship had been made. But she looked into the fire as though she had not heard him and made no reply.

'It's in pretty bad shape,' he went on. 'It'll want a bit of brass spending on it to make it comfortable. I had a good look round. I fancy extending it a bit besides modernising. I reckon I'd as soon live there as anywhere . . . I can't stop in a hotel for the rest of my life . . .'

She had resumed her hand-sewing and she went on with her work, not looking at him and not speaking. He was suddenly seized with the idea that she knew exactly what he was leading to and was only waiting for him to get to the point. But what would her reaction be? He glanced at her, uncertainly. Should he, so quickly? Perhaps he should wait until she had grown more used to having him about again? But time was slipping by. Neither of them was young and each of them was avoiding talking about the important things that concerned them both.

'Of course,' he said carefully, 'I shall need somebody to look after it for me . . . keep it tidy and cook . . .' He stopped for a moment, then went doggedly on. 'I know it'll seem a bit sudden-like after all this time, Sarah, but you know there's nobody I—'

He stopped again, alarmed this time, as Sarah stiffened in her chair, then stood up, her eyes flashing and all the smouldering antagonism he had felt before flaring openly.

'So it's housekeeping you're offering me after all these years, Morgan Lightly. Well if that's what's in your mind I'll tell you now that I need neither you nor your money. I wonder how you can find the face to come here as you do and expect me to fall in with your plans. I managed very well without you thirty years ago, and I can do the same now!'

'But, Sarah,' Morgan said, getting to his feet. 'You don't understand—'

'I understand well enough,' she said in a low, furious voice; 'and I want no part of it.' She turned her back on him and picked up the blouse she was sewing. 'Now if you don't mind, I've got work to do.'

Morgan stood there for a moment, frowning helplessly.

He could not make her out at all; and when she took no further notice of his presence he said good-bye and left.

Driving back to town he cursed himself for being a hasty fool and shook his head in wonder at the ways of women.

'I made a mess of it, Thomas,' he confided later, when sitting in the living-room over his brother's grocery shop in one of Cressley's dingy back streets. 'I should have bided my time. You can't step over thirty years as easy as all that.' He pulled thoughtfully at his pipe. 'But I can't understand why she flared up like that. I think she nearly hated me just then; as though I'd done her a wrong.'

'You touched her conscience, turning up like you did,' Thomas said. 'And I'm surprised at you, I must say, running to her of all people as soon as you get home. After what she did to you . . . Running off and marrying that chap the minute your back was turned, and you with it all fixed up for her to join you as soon as you got settled down a bit.'

Morgan sighed. 'Aye, but she was a grand lass, Thomas – and still is! A fine, proud woman. That's what's wrong with her – pride. If I could get round that I might do it yet. A fine woman . . . Just the comfort for a chap like me in the twilight of his days.'

'Twilight of your days!' Thomas scoffed. 'You want to go talking like that at your age! How old are you – fifty-two-three? And a fine upstanding chap with a bit of brass behind you. *You* shouldn't go short of comfort. There'll be plenty ready to see 'at you're comfortable. And a fat lot o' comfort *she* was to you. I never knew her well but I heard tell 'at you never knew which way she'd jump next.'

Morgan shook his head and smiled reflectively. 'I thought I knew, Thomas,' he said. 'I thought I knew, lad.'

Christmas came, and then the new year, bringing with it weeks of dry, biting winds; until February arrived, ferocious with driving snow and ice: a month in which there were periods when the temperature did not rise above freezing point for days together. And at last, when it seemed that the long grim winter was without end, the earth softened to the coming of spring. Catkins flickered like green light in the dark winter woods and crocuses appeared, white and mauve and yellow, in the public gardens of the town.

Morgan filled his days with the leisurely pleasures of looking up old friends and renewing old acquaintance-ships, and with his plans for making Greystone Cottage his home. His solitary home, it seemed now. For in all this time he had not seen Sarah once; but she was never far from his thoughts.

On a bright Sunday morning early in May he went as usual to Thomas's house for Sunday dinner. He found Meg, Thomas's wife, preparing the meal in the little kitchen over the shop.

'Thomas is up in the attic, Morgan,' she told him. 'He's taken it into his head to sort out some of his old belongings.'

Morgan climbed up into the top of the house and found his brother bending over a tin chest, looking through a collection of dusty books. He paused for a moment in the doorway and watched him. In the crouching attitude of that slight figure he saw for an instant the dreamy, bookish lad of long ago. Then, almost immediately, the spell was broken as Thomas straightened up and looked round.

'Oh, it's you, Morgan. Come in, come in.' The sunshine shafted down through the skylight and Thomas screwed up his eyes behind his glasses. 'I just bethought me to look at some of these old things of mine.'

Morgan sat down on a rickety chair and Thomas resumed his inspection of the dusty books, lifting them out one by one from the trunk, dusting them over, and peering at the titles. Occasionally he would stop and flip over the pages, reading a passage at random.

'I had a look at some of these the other week,' he said. 'First time I'd touched 'em in years.' He sat down on a box facing Morgan, a heavy, well-bound volume in his hands. 'Remember how I scraped and saved to buy these, Morgan? I did all manner of jobs.' He read out the title on the spine: '*A History of England and its People*, in ten volumes. I reckoned there couldn't be much history I wouldn't know if I read these.'

Morgan nodded. 'You were a rare lad for learning, Thomas.'

Thomas weighed the book in his hand. 'And now these books are a history in themselves, Morgan. My history: the history of a failure.'

He removed his glasses and cleaned the lenses on his handkerchief. 'It's funny the tricks life plays on you. When we were lads I was the one who was going to set the world on fire – me – Thomas, the scholar. Instead, I wind up keeping a back-street grocery shop, while you, the rough and ready lad, come back from the other side of the world with your fortune made, just like somebody in a book.'

In their youth the brothers had felt their dissimilarity too keenly for real closeness, but now Morgan felt a surge of affection for Thomas. 'You're too hard on yourself, lad,' he said gently. 'There's all kinds of failure and all kinds of success. You've been happy, haven't you? You've made Meg happy, I can see that. All I have to show for everything is a few quid in the bank. I'd be a liar and a hypocrite if I said that didn't matter. It's a great comfort, Thomas. But there are things I'd rather have had.'

Thomas smiled and touched Morgan's knee. 'I'm all right, Morgan. It's just you coming home that started me off thinking back. I'd not have had it any different – not if it had meant not having Meg.' He put the book aside and bent over the trunk. 'She'd skin me alive if she heard me talking like that.'

In a few minutes Meg came to the foot of the attic stairs and called them to lunch. Morgan put his pipe away and stood up to go.

'Just a minute, Morgan, before you go.'

Morgan turned and looked at his brother. Thomas, with a strange half-embarrassed expression on his thin face, was fumbling in his pocket. 'I've got something belonging to you that I think you should have.' He produced an envelope. 'It's been lying up here for years. I thought it was no good posting it on to you after all that time; but I couldn't bring myself to throw it away.'

He handed the envelope to Morgan, who took it and turned it over to look at the writing on it. There was no stamp, just his name in dried and faded ink.

'Well, what on earth is it?' he said.

'It's probably nothing much at all,' said Thomas. 'But it is yours and I think you should have it. Don't you know whose writing that is?'

'No.'

'It's hers – Sarah's. I reckon it was to tell you she wouldn't be coming out to you after all.'

Morgan made no move to open the envelope. 'Tell me, Thomas, just how you came by it.'

Thomas sat down again on the box.

'It was after you'd gone down to Southampton to see about your passage. I was coming down to see you off and visit Uncle Horace, remember? Well, you'd been gone a few days and Sarah gave me this to give to you. She was hanging about one night at the end of the street, waiting for me. I reckon she didn't know your address.' He shook his head and looked penitently at the floor. 'I don't know how it happened, Morgan, but what with one thing and another, I clean forgot it. I remember I wasn't too fit about that time. It was the year I cracked up and had to go into the sanatorium. Anyway, it wasn't till months later that I came across it again in a book. I reckoned if it had been all that important Sarah would have surely seen me to ask if you'd got it. As it was, by that time she was married to Mark what's his name and had a kiddy too. I saw no good reason for bothering any more. I know I'd no right to keep it back, but I reckoned you were well out of it.'

Morgan's eyes were fixed on his brother's face. 'And you mean you've hung on to it for thirty years?'

'Well, not exactly. I couldn't bring meself to burn somebody else's letter, you see, so I shoved it in a book again and I didn't come across it again till a week or two ago when I was rummaging about up here. I've been turning over in my mind ever since whether to give it to you and own up or destroy it and let sleeping dogs lie.'

Morgan ripped open the envelope and read the letter inside. Thomas stared at him as the colour drained from his face.

'For God's sake, Morgan, what is it, man?'

Morgan shook his head. 'Nothing, Thomas, nothing. It just brought it all back for a minute, that's all.'

He refolded the letter and returned it to the envelope which he put carefully away in an inside pocket. Of what use was it to rant and foam at Thomas now? As he had said, he was ill at the time, seriously ill and not to be held responsible for a careless mistake. And nothing would be gained by telling him now that this letter, delivered at the right time, could have changed the course of two people's lives.

'I . . . I am sorry, Morgan,' said Thomas, peering anxiously at his brother.

Morgan turned abruptly to the door. 'Forget it, Thomas,' he said. 'It was all a long time ago.'

They went downstairs as Meg called again. Throughout the meal Morgan was withdrawn and silent and it was not long after when he took his leave. Back at his hotel he sat down and wrote a note to Sarah. He thought for some time before putting pen to paper, and at length he wrote:

'My dear Sarah, The enclosed letter has only just come into my hands. It has explained many things to me and the fact that owing to a series of mischances my brother Thomas delivered it thirty years too late may help to ease what must have embittered you for so long . . .'

He put the note and Sarah's letter to him together in an envelope, and walking along to the corner by the hotel, he posted them in the pillar box there.

In the fine warm afternoon of the following Sunday Morgan visited Sarah for the first time in several months. There was a short pause before she answered his knock, and they regarded each other in silence for a long moment as she stood in her doorway.

'Well, Sarah,' Morgan said at last. 'I thought it was a nice day for a drive out.'

Her eyes were unfathomable as she said, 'I'll get a coat.'

He followed her into the house and was instantly drawn to the sideboard and the photograph of the young officer, Sarah's son. She returned suddenly to the room and her glance flickered briefly on his face as he stood there with the photograph in his hand.

'I'm ready.'

'Righto.' He replaced the picture on the sideboard and preceded her out of the house. Once clear of the narrow main street of the village, Morgan put on speed, heading straight for Greystone Cottage on which the work of conversion was now progressing. The hillside here was drenched in fresh green that was still untouched by the grimy smoke-fingers of industry which curled up out of the valley. In the orchard behind the house blossom sprang pink and white among the neglected trees. They walked in silence up the path and Morgan unlocked the door and stood aside for Sarah to enter. There was a new strangeness in their manner together now and they had spoken little in the car. From the cardboard tube he carried Morgan took out a copy of the architect's plan for the conversion. As they walked from room to room, striding over rubble and builders' materials, he explained to her all that was being done. She listened to him, nodding now and then, but making little comment. They came to the kitchen last of all and Morgan pointed to the tall cast-iron range and fireplace.

'That's going, Sarah. I'm knocking this wall right out and extending four feet back. There'll be all built-in units along that wall there. It's wonderful the things they make for kitchens nowadays.' He talked on, flourishing catalogues with shiny illustrations of gleaming kitchen equipment. 'It'll be fair dinkum when it's done.'

'Fair dinkum?'

'Australian for proper champion.'

'Oh.' She looked about her. 'Well, it sounds very nice.'

He watched her face with eagerness. 'Aye, it'll be labour-saving; and I reckon just enough for one woman to manage – with a bit of help for the heavy work, y'know.'

Sarah did not meet his eyes. 'You've got somebody in mind to look after it all for you, then?'

He gazed steadily at her. 'I think so, Sarah,' he said quietly. 'I'm thinking of getting married again. I know just the lass. She needs somebody to look after her.'

'Well, don't you think you should talk it over with her before you get it all settled? Especially the kitchen. Every woman has her ideas about kitchens.'

'Well, Sarah,' he said, 'let's have your ideas, then.'

'*My* ideas?'

'Whose ideas do you think they should be?'

She turned away from him, hiding her face and walking to the window which looked out on to the unkempt stretch of orchard.

'You know – you don't owe me anything, Morgan.'

'But look, Sarah—'

'He isn't yours, y'know.'

He was baffled now. He looked back at her with puzzlement in his eyes. 'I don't understand.'

'John, I mean,' Sarah said. She stood quite still, looking out of the window, both hands clasping her bag. 'He's not your boy, Morgan.'

'I . . . I don't understand, Sarah,' he said again. 'The letter . . .'

'Oh, that was true enough.' She turned and walked aimlessly across the gritty floorboards, not looking at him. He watched her, his eyes never leaving her as she said, 'It never came to anything. I was mistaken. John is Mark's boy, Morgan, not yours.' She looked at him now, watching for his reaction as he lifted his hands in a gesture of helplessness.

'I don't know what to think now, Sarah. For a week I've believed I had a son.' He smiled wanly. 'It wasn't a bad feeling.

'And what about Mark? You married him just the same.'

'I was panic-stricken,' Sarah said. She gazed past his shoulder with the look of one who sees not great distances but over the long passage of years. 'I didn't know which way to turn. I thought you'd let me down. I told Mark. He'd always wanted me.'

Morgan nodded. 'I know.'

'And he still wanted me after I'd told him. I was afraid and lost. I didn't know what to do. Mark seemed the only way out.'

'But you found you were mistaken?'

'Yes, soon enough. But I couldn't give Mark up then, not after he'd stood by me. So we were married. I didn't love him – not the way I'd loved you – but I respected him. He was such a good man, such a kind and gentle man that I couldn't help but come to love him in time. We had a good life together: a good marriage. And we had John.'

'And all these years you've been thinking that I'd let you down?' Morgan said.

She smiled dryly. 'And you've been thinking the same of me.'

'Oh, what a waste,' he burst out. 'What a wicked, wicked waste!'

'No, Morgan, not a waste. We both brought happiness to someone else. It wasn't a waste.'

He rolled the plans in his hands. 'No, you're right.'

She straightened her back and strolled across the room again. 'So you're not obliged to me after all, Morgan. You don't owe me anything.'

'No, we're quits,' Morgan said. 'We're back where we started.'

'Except we're both thirty years older,' Sarah pointed out; 'and we've both been married.'

'Which is no reason for not having another go.'

'It's not everybody that wants another go,' she said. 'Some people are satisfied with what they've had.' She turned to face him. 'I don't *have* to get married. I'm quite comfortable as I am. I have my pension and my sewing and John sends me money. I'm self-sufficient, y'know.'

Morgan nodded. 'Aye, it'd take more than being widowed to get you down.'

'But it's not that nobody wants me. I'm young enough, y'know, and not bad looking. I've had my chances.'

Morgan began to smile. 'I don't doubt it lass. But don't you think it was a happy providence that kept you till I'd come right round the world for you?'

'Right round the world for me? To your old Yorkshire, you mean!'

'But only a Yorkshire with you in it, Sarah. If I hadn't known you were a widow I don't think I'd have come at all.'

She tossed her head suddenly and in the coquettish gesture he saw quite clearly the girl he had loved and lost so long ago.

G

'Nay,' she said, 'you'll have to convince me of that.'

He slapped the cardboard tube down in his hand, laughing out loud. His heart sang.

'I will, lass,' he said. 'By God, but I will!'

And he did.

THE DESPERADOES

WHAT started it that night was the row Vince had with his father. He couldn't remember just what began the row itself, but something like it seemed to blow up every time the Old Man saw him, and started using expressions like 'idle layabout,' 'lazy good-for-nothing' and 'no-good little teddy boy.' The Old Man never talked to you – he talked at you; he didn't carry on a conversation – he told you things. When Vince stormed out of the house he hardly knew where he was going he was so full of bottled-up fury. Violence writhed in him like a trapped and vicious snake. He felt like kicking in the teeth of the first person who might glance twice at him and he thought that perhaps the easiest way of relieving his feelings would be to find the boys and go smash up a few chairs at the Youth Club. Except that that might bring a copper to the door and he got on the wrong side of the Old Man easily enough without having the police to help along.

He had no trouble in finding the gang: they were obstructing the pavement at the end of Chapel Street, making the occasional passer-by get off into the road. He watched them sourly as he descended the hill – stocky Sam, little Finch, and big surly Bob – and his mouth twisted peevishly as he heard one of them laugh. They were watching something across the road that he could not see and they did not notice his approach till he was upon them.

'Now then.'

'What ho!'

'How do, Vince.'

Sam said, 'Get a load of that,' nodding across the junction.

Vince looked. He might have known. It was a girl. She was straddling a drop-handlebar bicycle by the kerb and talking to a thin youth who stood on the edge of the pavement. She was a dark blonde. She wore very brief scarlet shorts which displayed her long, handsome thighs, and a white high-necked sweater stretched tight over her large shapely breasts.

Finch was hopping about as though taken bad for a leak and making little growling noises in his throat.

'D'you know her?' Vince asked.

'Never seen her before.'

'Who's that Sunday-school teacher with her?'

'Don't know him either.'

Vince felt a spasm of gratuitous hatred for the youth. There was no one about; the street was quiet in the early evening. He said, 'Well, what we waitin' for? Let's see him off, eh?'

'An' what then?' Bob said.

Vince looked at him where he lounged against the lamp-post, his hands deep in the pockets of his black jeans. He was becoming more and more irritated by Bob's habit of making objections to everything he suggested. He had a strong idea that Bob fancied taking over leadership of the gang but lacked the guts to force the issue.

'What d'you mean "what then?" ?' he said.

There was no expression on Bob's long sullen face. 'When we've seen him off?'

'We'll take her pants off an' make her ride home bare-back,' Finch giggled.

'Aye,' Vince said; 'an' if laughing boy has any objections we'll carve his initials round his belly button.'

He brought his hand out of his pocket and pushed the handle of his knife against Bob's shirt front just above the buckle of his belt. He pressed the catch and let his relaxed wrist take the spring of the blade. He wondered if anyone had ever made a knife with a spring strong enough to drive the blade straight into a man's belly.

'You want to be careful wi' that bloody thing,' Bob said, eyeing the six inches of razor-sharp steel, its point pricking one of the pearl buttons on his black shirt. 'Don't you know there's a law against 'em?'

'I'll have to be careful who sees me with it, then, won't I?' Vince said. Looking Bob in the eye he inclined his head across the street. 'Comin'?' he said.

Bob shrugged with exaggerated casualness and eased his shoulders away from the lamp-post as Vince retracted the blade of the knife. 'Okay; may as well.'

They crossed the road in a tight group, fanning out as they neared the opposite side to approach the girl and the youth from two sides. The youth looked more startled than the girl to see them coming.

'Hello, sweetheart,' Vince said. 'Been for a ride in the country?'

Finch rang the bell on the bike's handlebars. 'Your mam's ringing for you,' he said to the youth. 'Time you were off home.'

The youth looked confused and startled. His smooth, unshaven cheeks flared with a brilliant flush of red as he looked at the faces of the gang.

'What's all this about?' the girl said, and the youth, finding voice, said, 'Why don't you go away and leave people alone?'

'Why don't you go away an' leave *us* alone?' Vince said. He waved his hand at the youth. 'Go on, sonny, get lost. Beat it.'

Sam, Finch and Bob closed round the youth and began to hustle him away along the street. 'Let me alone. Who d'you think you are?' he said as they moved him along. They turned a corner with him into a side street and his voice died away. Vince held the handlebars of the bicycle with one hand to prevent the girl from leaving.

She flashed blue eyes at him. 'Who d'you think you are,' she said, echoing the youth, 'pushing people around like this?'

'Vice squad,' Vince said. 'Cleaning the streets up.'

'Well you want to start by staying at home yourselves.'

'Now that's not nice, is it?' Vince said. 'After we've protected you from that creep.'

'He's not a creep.' The girl's eyes flashed over him, taking in the long pepper-and-salt jacket, the exaggeratedly narrow black trousers, the black shirt, opennecked, with stand-up collar, and the white triangle of sweat shirt at the throat. Vince in his turn was examining her with appreciation: the spirited blue eyes in a lightly tanned face, the shapely breasts taut under the sweater, the long bare legs.

'He's a creep,' he said. 'You're the best-looking piece of crackling I've seen in a fortnight. What you want to waste your time with a drip like that for?'

'It's a question of taste,' the girl said coldly. She looked back over her shoulder at the empty street. 'What are they doing to him? I'm warning you, if they hurt him I'll report you all to the police. Don't think you can frighten me.'

'Oh, they won't hurt him,' Vince said. 'They'll just see him on his way.'

As he spoke, Sam and Finch and Bob reappeared round the corner. Finch was laughing and saying something to the others.

'Where is he?' the girl said. 'What have you done to him?'

'We didn't lay a finger on him,' Sam said. 'All done by kindness.'

'He's remembered he's got to do an errand for his mother,' Finch said with a snigger.

'And I've got to go as well,' the girl said. 'Would you mind taking your hand off the handlebars?'

'What's the hurry,' Vince said, 'just when we're gettin' friendly?'

Finch was prowling round the bike, pretending to examine it. He crouched beside the front wheel and fingered the tyre valve.

'Is this where the air goes in an' out?'

'Don't you touch that!' the girl said.

'No, leave it alone, Finch,' said Vince.

'Thank you for nothing.'

'Isn't she polite?' Vince asked the others. 'She must have been to a good school.'

'Where d'you live, love?' Sam asked.

'Not far from here. And you'd better let me go if you know what's good for you. My father's a sergeant in the police force.'

'An' my old man's the chief constable,' Vince said; 'so they'll know one another. What's your name?'

'None of your business.'

'That's a funny name,' said Finch, and the gang hooted with laughter that was mostly forced.

Vince was wishing the others had stayed away longer, because he was sure he could have made some progress with her, given more time. All this defiance – it was mostly show. She was just keeping her end up and he wondered what she was like behind it, when you got to know her.

'P'raps we'd better introduce ourselves,' he said with a little bow. He pointed to Sam. 'That's Sir Walter Raleigh;' to Finch: 'Field Marshal Montgomery;' to Bob: 'Marilyn Monroe in disguise; an' I'm Sammy Davis, junior.'

'Very funny,' the girl said. 'Now I'll thank you to let me go.'

'Tell us your name an' then we'll see.'

'I've told you, it's none of your business.'

'I used to know a lad called nobody's business,' Finch said, pursuing his joke. 'Was he your brother? Then there was one called dirty business – the black sheep of the family.'

Vince was watching the girl's face closely. Was that really the faintest flicker of humour in the depths of her eyes, or was he imagining things?

'Well, if you won't tell us, we'll have to keep you a bit longer. Can't let you go when you're feeling so unfriendly.'

'Look,' she said, 'if you don't let me go I'll call out to that man over there.'

Vince smiled. 'He'd probably run like hell the other way. You read every day in the papers about people gettin' hurt through not minding their own business.'

'Proper young gentlemen, all of you,' the girl said. She gave a quick backward look over her shoulder. 'Well I don't think you'll scare two policemen.'

They all fell for it. Vince said, 'What . . .?' and as he momentarily relaxed his grip on the handlebars she sent

Finch reeling from a swift push in the chest and pressing down on the pedals, was away.

She swayed uncertainly for a moment as she forced the speed, and then she was gone, head down, scarlet shorts brilliant in the drab street.

'Fancy fallin' for that one,' said Sam.

Vince watched until she turned the bend and disappeared from sight. 'She's a real smart piece,' he said. 'You've got to give her that . . . A real smart piece.' He found himself hoping he would meet her again in more favourable circumstances and he let his mind dwell briefly on her remembered charms.

'I could shag it from supper to breakfast-time,' said little Finch, and Sam laughed and punched him tauntingly on the shoulder.

'Aagh, she'd make mincemeat o' two your size,' he scoffed. 'It takes a man, mate, a man.'

'Just gimme the chance,' Finch said. 'I'd risk it.'

'Here,' Bob said all at once, 'what did you mean by sayin' I was Marilyn Monroe in disguise? You tryin' to make out I'm a puff or summat?'

'I just said the first thing 'at came into me head,' Vince said.

'Well why didn't you say it about Finch or Sam? Why me?'

There was a dangerous little smile lurking in Vince's eyes as he looked at Bob. 'I just didn't think of it till I got to you.'

'Well I didn't like it. You want to be careful.'

'Or else what?' Vince said nastily, his temper flaring again. 'Are you tryin' to make summat out o' summat?'

'I'm just tellin' you,' Bob said.

'That's your trouble: you're allus tellin'. What's up –

don't you like runnin' around with this gang, or what?'

'I like it okay.'

'Well why don't you shurrup allus tellin' an' objectin' every time anybody says anythin' or suggests anythin'?'

'I'm just sayin' what I think,' Bob said. 'Seems there's only one what does any suggestin' round here.'

Vince felt himself go tense. There, it was out, it was said. 'Meanin' what?' he said.

'Meanin' everything you say goes an' nobody else has a look in.'

Vince kept his eyes levelled on Bob's face and slowly slid his hands free of his pockets.

'I haven't heard anybody else objectin'.'

'Oh no, they'll fall in with owt you say.'

'Well that makes you the odd man out. You're outnumbered, three to one.'

'Why don't you belt up, Bob?' Sam said. 'What you want to start all this for?'

'I'm only sayin' what I think,' Bob said, his heavy face flushed now.

Vince, watching him, knew that the moment, if there was to be one, was not now. 'Well now you've said it.'

'Aye . . . well . . . I can say what I think, can't I?'

'Course you can,' Vince said. 'Any time.' He clapped Bob on the shoulder and threw his other arm round Sam's neck.

'Well, now Bob's said his piece, what we goinna do, eh?'

'Let Bob suggest summat,' Sam said. 'He's grumbled enough.'

'That's it,' Vince said. 'What we goinna do, Bob?'

Bob looked surly. 'I don't know.'

'There's that stripper on at the Tivvy,' Finch said,

prancing round from behind them. 'I've seen the pictures outside.' He drew a voluptuous torso in the air with his hands. 'Grrr.'

'We could go up to the Troc or the Gala Rooms after an' find some women,' Sam said.

'They mebbe won't let us in at the Gala Rooms after last week,' Vince said, referring to a fight they had been involved in on the dance floor.

'An' there's Jackson at the Troc,' Bob reminded them.

'Aw, he's got nowt on us,' Sam said. 'He won't keep us out.'

'That big, stupid, brussen, show-off bastard,' Vince said. 'One o' these days somebody'll walk all over his stupid face, an' I want to be there when it happens so's I can have a good laugh.'

'Well what say we go to the Tivvy first an' then the Troc?' Sam suggested, and Vince nodded.

'Aye, let's go to the Tivvy first an' give Finch a thrill.'

'Here, why me?' Finch said. 'Anybody 'ud think you lot didn't like tarts.'

'As I says to the vicar the other night, over our glass of dandelion wine,' Vince began. 'I says, "Vicar," I says, "I don't know what we're goinna do about young Finch. He's got women on the brain, Vicar, an' he keeps his brains in his trousers, y'know . . ."'

'Come off it,' Finch said.

Vince grinned and winked at Sam and they seized Finch and turned him upside down, holding him by the ankles, his head six inches from the pavement. Coins fell out of his pockets as he wriggled furiously.

'Lay off, you bloody fools. Stop yer bloody clownin'!'

'Have we to get it out an' cool it off, Sam?' Vince said, pretending to fumble at Finch's flies.

'You bloody dare!' Finch roared.

'He might catch cold in it,' Sam said; 'an' that'd never do.'

Finch put his hands flat down on the pavement as they lowered him. They released his legs and stood by laughing as he righted himself and then scurried about the pavement retrieving his loose change. Vince clapped him on the shoulder and pulled him in between Sam and himself.

'C'mon, then; let's go an' have a belly laugh an' a look at this tart.'

They caught a downtown bus and sat in a noisy group on the upper deck. They got off at the corner of Market Street. The Tivoli theatre stood in an alley near the centre of town. It was very small and, now that the Alhambra had closed its doors, the only live theatre in Cressley. It boasted, along with the City Varieties, Leeds, of being one of the oldest music halls in the country and in its time it had played host to all the legendary names of variety. But its hey-day was far behind it. It could not compete with the mass audiences and huge fees available on television and it was fifteen years since any important name had appeared on its playbills. The fare it offered now was a series of fifth-rate touring shows composed of those who had never made the top, the pathetically hopeful, and strip-tease artistes and semi-nude performers of varying ages, talent, and physical charm. The gang paused to examine with lewd and vociferous admiration the photographs of Paula Perez, the Peruvian Peach, displayed in the foyer.

'Four on the stage,' Vince said to the woman in the box.

She glanced at the seating plan. 'Four orchestra stalls, row G, at four-and-six,' she recited, without smiling. 'First house just starting.'

They paid and went in, ignoring the programme-seller just inside the door, and marched down the side aisle of the narrow red-plush auditorium. The hall was almost full near the front, but the audience thinned out noticeably towards the rear. They stumbled without apology over the feet of the people already seated as the five-piece pit band struck up, the steely tone of the violin characteristically dominating the sound. The curtains parted and five young women with frozen smiles went through a lackadaisical routine of slipshod precision dancing.

'Cor,' Finch said, 'lamp that elephant on the end.'

'Must be the producer's daughter,' Vince said.

'Looks more like his mother,' Sam said.

They began to clap loudly and shout ' 'Core, 'core,' as the dancers tripped in line off the stage.

Their place was taken by a perky, broadly smiling young man in a light grey suit, blue polka-dot bow tie and a soft hat with the brim turned up all round. He peered over the footlights, pretending to look for the audience.

'Is anybody there?'

'There's only thee an' me,' Vince called out.

The comedian responded with a quick professional grin. 'An' there'll awnly be thee in a minute,' he retorted in an imitation Yorkshire accent.

Finch nearly fell out of his seat laughing at this. He leaned forward and thumped the back of the seat in front, causing the little nondescript man in glasses sitting there to turn and give him a glare.

The comedian was also the compere. He told a couple of stories to warm up the audience, then introduced the first act: a saxophone and xylophone duo.

The first half of the show moved on through an acrobatic trio, a young singing discovery from Scotland, a brother-and-sister tap-dancing act, interspersed with quips, stories and lightning impersonations from the compere, and came to its climax with Paula Perez the Peruvian Peach. Peruvian or not, she was black-haired, dark-eyed and brown-skinned. She performed against a pale mauve back-curtain, with a dressing-table, a cheval mirror and a double divan bed as props. She began in a dark mauve cocktail dress, and elbow-length white gloves which she peeled slowly off and held at arm's length before dropping them in turn on to the stage. To the music of the orchestra she turned her back and unzipped her frock. She stepped gracefully out of it with a coy backward glance at the audience and performed a few steps about the stage in a transparent nylon slip. The gang were still and absorbed now, except Finch, who fidgeted restlessly in his seat as though impatient for each succeeding move in the sequence of disrobing. The slip went, followed by the stockings, which were shed with much waving of long legs from the depths of a bedside chair. Miss Perez now went into an extended dance routine in which her long legs flashed and the mounds of her breasts quivered and trembled above the low line of her white brassiere. She turned her back to the audience once more and unhooked the brassiere, throwing it away from her on to the bed. Turning again, she continued the dance with her arms crossed over her breasts, finally turning her back yet again while she ridded herself of her transparent pants. The act was almost over. The audience waited for the climax that would reveal all. The Peruvian Peach moved a few steps each way, her dimpled buttocks quivering, then stopped in the middle of the stage. For a long moment she did not move. A side-drum rolled in the orchestra pit. Suddenly she spun round, flinging her arms wide. The pale rose of her nipples and the triangle of diamanté-studded cloth in the vee of her thighs were visible for a split second before the stage lights were doused.

She stepped between the curtains in a lilac-coloured nylon négligé to receive the applause of the audience, blowing kisses and flashing her dark, mascara-ed eyes into every corner of the house.

Finch thumped the back of the seat in front in his excitement, and the little man turned his head.

'Do you mind?' he said. 'I've paid for this seat.'

Finch gave him a blank look and went on applauding wildly until the Peruvian Peach had disappeared from the stage.

They made their way out to the stalls bar and extolled the charms of Paula Perez while they drank bottled beer.

'Does she come on again in the second half?' Finch asked.

'They usually do,' Vince said.

'I wonder what she'll do this time.'

'Ask for a volunteer to go up an' unfasten her clothes for her.'

'Gerraway!' Finch said, his eyes popping at the thought.

They had a second bottle of beer apiece, the quick intake of alcohol loosening in them a pleasant sense of irresponsibility and a desire for some mischief to add spice to the entertainment offered.

'See that little bloke in front o' me gettin' an eyeful?' Finch said.

'What did he say when he turned round?' Vince asked.

'Oh, summat about me keepin' to me own seat.'

Vince raised his eyebrows. 'Did he, then? We might have a bit o' sport with him before we've done.'

They returned to their seats as the band struck up. The

show sagged in its second half and Vince soon became bored and restless through the repeat sequence of acts. As the acrobats bounded on to the stage he snapped open his knife and pushed the blade through the red plush upholstery between his thighs. He ripped open a slit six inches long and probed for the stuffing, pulling out a handful and passing it to Finch on his left. 'Here, hold that for me, will you?' Finch dropped the wadding on to the floor, consumed by a fit of giggling. There was an empty seat immediately in front of Vince and to the right of the nondescript man who had spoken to Finch. Vince put the knife away and lit a cigarette and leaned forward to expel smoke about the little man's ears. The man coughed and looked round. Vince showed his teeth in a smile and the little man turned away in some confusion. Eventually, after repeated references to it by the comedian-compere, it was the turn once more of Paula Perez. She assumed the role of a slave-girl, with a loin cloth and a strip of matching material across her breasts, dancing before a painted wooden idol which stood at the back of the stage. The curtain fell when she had prostrated herself in an attitude of abandon before the idol, and rose again almost immediately to show the Peruvian Peach concealed behind two large ostrich-feather fans. She had disposed of the garments worn during the slave-girl act and as she danced now the manipulation of the fans allowed the audience momentary glimpses of her naked, made-up body.

Vince leaned forward and spoke into the ear of the little man:

'You're a dirty old man comin' here to look at women's tits when you should be at home puttin' the kids to bed. Look at her, though – she's got a lovely pair, hasn't she? Isn't she a teasing bitch the way she gives you just a look an' no more? I bet you're wondering what she's like in bed, aren't you, eh? Wouldn't you like to fondle 'em, eh? Run your hands all over her . . .'

The little man eased over to the far side of his seat, his gaze fixed on the stage and the Peruvian Peach. Vince went on talking, his suggestions becoming more and more obscene, and the little man began to sweat, small beads of perspiration breaking on his forehead and running down his fleshy cheeks. Until, as Paula Perez reached the climax of her act, where she retired to the back of the stage, dropped the fans and froze into a nude pose, his nerve broke and he left his seat and stumbled along the row to the aisle.

Vince waited for a moment before nudging Sam on his right. 'Go on, get out, quick!' Sam, not knowing quite what Vince was up to, did as he was told and with Finch and Bob following they left the theatre and paused in the brightly lit foyer.

'What's all the rush about?' said Bob. 'It wasn't over.'

'All bar the shoutin'. C'mon.' Vince led the way to the end of the cobbled alley and stopped, looking right and left along the street. 'He's there.' The little man was crossing the road, walking fast, about twenty yards away.

'C'mon, we're goinna have a bit o' sport.'

They crossed over the street, following the man but keeping some distance behind him. Once he glanced back as though expecting to be followed, then hurried on, his pace not slackening. In a short while he had left the main thoroughfares and was striking up the hill into the back streets. They saw him turn a corner and, turning it after him, found him thirty yards away, alone in a dimly lit street running between two sheer-sided blocks of mill offices. Vince called after him:

H

'Ey! you there; wait for us!'

The man stopped only to look back; then he began to run.

'C'mon,' Vince said.

'What we goinna do?' Bob said.

'We're goinna have some *fun*.'

He broke into a fast run, the others following. They easily outpaced the little man and overtook him well within the confines of the lonely street. He backed against a wall as they reached him.

'What's wrong?' he said. 'What d'you want?'

'We just wanted to talk to you,' Vince said. They faced him in an arc and he fought for breath, his chest heaving, as his frightened glance flickered from face to face.

'What about? I'm in a hurry.'

'Dashin' off to tell the missis all about Paula Perez an' her marvellous tits,' Vince said.

'There's no call for mucky talk like that,' the man said.

'Don't tell me,' Vince said. 'I know – you're an art-lover. I bet you like mucky photos an' all. Have you any on you now? C'mon, show us your mucky photos.'

'I don't know what you're talking about.' The lenses of the little man's glasses flickered dimly as his eyes turned to look at each face in turn. 'Can't a man have a quiet evening at the theatre on his own without being molested by hooligans?'

'Hooligans? Hear that, lads? He says we're hooligans.' Vince took hold of the man's coat. 'Let's see them mucky pictures.'

'I haven't *got* any mucky pictures. Now let me go or I'll shout for help.'

'I wouldn't do that if I were you,' Vince told him. 'That wouldn't be friendly at all.'

'Well let me go, then. I don't know what you want. I haven't done anything to you.'

'Who says you have?'

'Nobody, but—'

'Well, what you bindin' about, then?'

'Look, all I want is to get on about my own business, that's all.'

Vince let go of the man's coat and appeared to consider this. He looked at his friends in turn. 'He wants to get on about his business. Shall we let him?'

'Yes, let's let him,' Sam said.

'Even though he's called us hooligans?'

'Well, he doesn't know us,' Sam said. 'Anybody can make a mistake.'

'We don't want to take it out of him over a little mistake, do we?' Vince said. He stepped away from the little man, allowing him to move clear of the wall. Vince extended his hand. 'No hard feelings, eh?' The little man looked at Vince's hand before putting out his own to meet it. As Vince grasped, he pulled, jerking the little man forward so that he staggered against him. 'Been drinkin' an' all,' Vince said. 'A bit unsteady on your feet, aren't you? Mebbe a spot o' shut-eye 'ud do you good.'

With no more warning he smashed his fist into the man's face, sending him reeling backwards to fall over Sam, who had taken up a crouching position behind him. The man rolled over, face down, and groaned, his hands moving feebly. Sniggering, Finch danced on the fallen spectacles, the lenses crunching under his shoes. As the man moved and made as if to lift himself on his hands, Bob moved in and drove his foot into his ribs. He collapsed again and lay still.

'Let's blow,' Vince said.

Bob looked round from where he was bending over the man. 'What about his wallet? He might have some brass on him.'

'Leave it,' Vince said sharply. 'We don't want pinchin' for robbery with violence. Not unless it's big enough to make it worth the risk.'

They left the scene, cutting out of the street by way of a ginnel and returning to the middle of town by a round-about route. They went into the saloon bar of a public house, ordered pints of bitter and sat down at a corner table. As he drank, Vince relived the moment when the sight of the little man's stupid face had become unbearable and felt again the violent uncoiling of tension in the smash of his fist. The violence had given them all a sense of release and now they talked animatedly about the show and Paula Perez, and women in general. Another two rounds of drinks increased their feeling of well-being and they decided it was time to go to the Trocadero and try their luck. They felt ready for anything, even to face the arch-enemy, Jackson.

He was standing in the foyer, eyeing everyone going in, his hard, square-jawed face expressionless. He wore a light blue double-breasted suit which hung easily on his big muscular body. He moved across to the pay-box as Vince and the others stepped in from the street.

'Hello, hello. What's up – won't they let you in at the Gala Rooms?'

'Why, what d'you mean?' Vince asked blandly.

'Don't come the injured innocence with me,' Jackson said. 'You know there was a scrap there last week.'

'Nothin' to do with us, Mister Jackson,' Finch said.

'Well I'm paid to keep order here,' Jackson said stonily;

'and the first sign of trouble here tonight and you lot are out. Just bear it in mind.'

He nodded to the girl in the box and she took their money and issued tickets. He watched them bleakly as they filed past him into the hall.

'Bastard,' Vince said as they passed through the doorway and out of earshot.

They edged their way through the press of people standing just inside the doors and stood on the edge of the floor to watch the dancers with cool, dangerous insolence on their young faces. An archway on the left led through the trellised wall to the coffee and soft drinks bar. Vince said, 'We'll meet over there between sets.' It was routine to them to have a gathering-place as they liked to know where support lay in case of trouble. Before they could separate now Finch grabbed Vince's arm in excitement.

'Ey, look who's there.'

'Where?' Vince said. 'Who?'

'That tart on the bike. Christ, look at her! What a dish! Over there, see, dancin' with that tall lad in the blue sports coat.'

Vince found her and as his gaze fell on her something in him seemed to turn over. She was wearing a wide, blue-flowered skirt topped by a sheer nylon blouse through which was visible the lace edging of her slip. He rubbed his hands together. His palms were already hot and moist from the heat of the hall.

'That's for me.'

'Ey up!' Finch said. 'I saw her first, din' I?'

'Get lost, laddie,' Vince told him. 'Go find somebody your own measure.'

He began to edge along the perimeter of the floor, formed at this end of the hall by the people standing, and farther down towards the bandstand by the green cane chairs set out along the wall under the curtained windows. The set ended, the floor clearing, and he found the girl standing with her partner, the tall youth in blue sports coat and grey slacks. Vince took his measure as he approached, decided he did not constitute any serious threat, and greeted the girl boldly:

'Well, well, well! Fancy running into you here! Got home all right, did you? No punctures or anything?'

The girl's glance was momentarily startled, then cool. 'Yes, thank you very much.'

'Good,' Vince said, smiling broadly now. 'Good.' He looked into the eyes of the tall youth. 'What's your name, might I ask?'

The young man's eyebrows came together. 'Colin Norton. Why?'

'I thought it was. There's somebody askin' for you up at the door.'

'Oh? Who is it?'

'Dunno. Young bloke; wavy hair.'

The tall young man pondered this for a moment. 'I'd better go and see . . .' He looked uncertainly from Vince to the girl. 'Excuse me.'

'Sure,' Vince said.

He watched Norton walk up the hall, then turned back to the girl. 'You with him?'

'No, not particularly.'

'Did you come with anybody else?'

'I've one or two friends here.'

'Boy friends?'

She shrugged faintly. 'Nobody special.'

Vince grinned. 'Go-od.'

'Was there really somebody asking for him?'

Vince's smile broadened. 'You never know.'

She began to smile in turn. It broke through first in her eyes, then moving her mouth.

'You're a proper devil, aren't you?'

'That's me,' Vince said. 'Right first time.'

He was pleased when the band struck up again. He wanted to be away from this spot before Norton realised he had been hoaxed. Not that he couldn't take care of him if it came to that, but he didn't want any trouble to complicate matters now. He jerked his head in the direction of the floor, which was filling up again.

'Care to?'

She hesitated, her glance flickering up to his face.

'All right.'

It was a slow foxtrot. He took her lightly in his arms, keeping the correct distance, and steered her with easy confidence through the moving throng of dancers. When they had made one circuit of the floor she said, 'You're a very good dancer, you know.'

Vince nodded. 'I know. It comes easy. If you're light on your feet and have a sense of rhythm there's nothing to it. Practice helps . . . You're not so bad yourself, anyway.'

'I'm better if I have a good partner. Half these lads can hardly dance a step. They grab hold of you like a sack of potatoes and walk all over your feet . . .'

'No style,' Vince said, 'that's their trouble.'

She gave him a quick speculative look, but said nothing. He pulled her in a little closer.

'I don't even know your name.'

'I know yours; you're Sammy Davis, junior.'

'That's only my professional name. Vincent Elspey's my real name.'

'I like that. It sounds a bit distinguished.'

'My friends call me Vince.'

'Do they? How nice for them.'

He didn't know what to make of this so he said nothing for a minute, waiting.

'Well?'

'Well what?'

'What's your name? I can't talk to you all night without knowing your name, can I?'

'Are you thinking of talking to me all night?'

'That and other things.'

She pulled away and looked at him. 'Just a minute! Not so fast, friend. I think you've got your lines crossed somewhere. Don't be getting ideas.'

'What ideas?'

'You know what ideas.'

'Cross my heart,' Vince said.

'And what?'

'I mean every word I say.'

She laughed again, as earlier, almost despite herself, the light coming to her dark blue eyes, the smile lifting the corners of her red mouth.

'Come on,' Vince said. 'What's your name?'

She shook her head.

'Come on. What's wrong?'

'I don't like it.'

'What?'

'My name.'

'Well what is it?'

She hesitated. 'Iris.'

'Well what's wrong with that, for Pete's sake?'

'I don't know. I just don't like it.'

'It's okay. What's wrong with it? I thought you were goinna say Aggie or Clara or summat right horrible.'

'Oh, no. I just don't like it, though. I've always wished I was called something else.'

'Such as what, for instance?'

'Well, Audrey, or something like that.'

'Well then, we'll reckon you never told me your real name an' I'll call you Audrey. How about that?'

'All right.'

He saw Sam standing alone on the edge of the floor and caught his eye, lifting his hand from the girl's back to form an 'O' with forefinger and thumb. He winked over the girl's shoulder and Sam gave him an approving wink in return and the thumbs-up sign. Sam was the one Vince was closest to in the gang. He had known him longer than the others and he was a good lad to have beside you in a tight corner. Little Finch was okay but his size meant that he couldn't throw much weight into a fight; and Bob, big enough and tough when it came right down to it, spent half his time sulking because somebody had hurt his feelings.

When the second of the three dances in the set ended he asked the girl if she would like a cup of coffee. She said she didn't mind and they went through into the snack bar adjoining the floor.

'Where are your friends tonight?' she asked when they were seated, with cups of coffee on the green Formica-topped table between them.

'Here.'

'Do you always run around with the same crowd?'

'Usually. You have your own mates, y'know.'

'Do you always go about looking for trouble?'

'What d'you mean?'

'Oh, come on,' she said. 'You know the way you hustled John Sharpe off tonight.'

'Was that his name?'

'Yes. Do you always do just what you want like that?'

He didn't like the question. He felt a lack of the power of argument necessary to defend his position. And anyway, all that had no part in this, sitting here with her. He remembered again the moment when he had driven his fist into the face of the man in the back street and felt no shame, because that part of him, the part keyed to violence, was separate from the part which sat here enjoying being with her. She was waiting for him to say something.

'We like a bit o' fun,' he said reluctantly.

'Fighting as well?'

'We have a scrap now an' again.' He glanced at her face. 'Well, you can't back down if somebody starts throwin' his weight about, can you?'

'But you never pick fights with anybody? You don't start trouble?'

'Look,' he said, 'you've got to have a bit o' fun. You've got to break out now and again. You'd go barmy if you didn't. You spend all day workin' to fill somebody else's pockets with brass, an' everybody allus on to you: the Old Man callin' you a layabout an' a ted, an' the coppers watching you when you cross the road because your hair's cut a bit different. They're all alike: they want everything their way. Just be quiet an' don't get under the feet. Don't get in the way. An' what sort of a mess have they all made of it, eh? Wars an' bombs 'at'll kill everybody if they let 'em off. An' they say, "Keep quiet, don't cause trouble. Just keep out of the way till we're ready to polish you off." '

His fist clenched itself on the table-top. 'Sometimes you feel you just can't rest till you've smashed summat; till you've shown 'em all you don't give a bugger for any of 'em, an' they can't boss you around.'

She sat very still, listening to him, her eyes on his face.

'Suppose everybody thought like you?' she said. 'What sort of world would it be then?'

'Couldn't be much worse than it is now, could it? Nobody trusts anybody. Everybody's out to get what he wants. Countries as well as people. Well I haven't got it upstairs – what it takes to make myself a nice little pile, like some of 'em do; so people look at me as if I'm dirt an' say, "Look at him, a ted, goin' about making trouble." So I make trouble when I feel like it.'

'But what about the ordinary decent people?'

'You mean the stupid ones, the ones everybody puts on? They're the ones the coppers an' politicians push around. Suckers. They're okay till nobody wants 'em. Like our old feller. He goes an' gets himself all shot up in the war an' now he's got one arm what's practically useless. So he gets a bit of a pension an' does jobs nobody else wants and walks about with it all twisted up inside him, hating everybody, including me, because I've got two good arms an' I can earn more brass than he does. An' he calls me a layabout!'

He drained his cup and pushed it moodily aside. 'What you want to start all that for? Why d'you want to bring all that up?'

She looked down into her own cup. 'I just wanted to know about you.'

They sat in silence for a time, then he said abruptly, 'C'mon, let's go dance some more.'

He stood aside at the door to let her precede him and as he followed her he noticed for the first time a small wart on the back of her neck, just below the hair-line. The lights were down in the hall for a slow waltz and, curiously touched by the blemish he had just noticed, he tightened his hold as they moved away together and brought her closer until her hair was touching his cheek. He wondered where she lived and if she would let him see her home when the dance finished. He wanted this very much. He wanted to see her again afterwards, too, and knew he would ask her for a date before long. She wasn't like the girls he and the gang usually went for: she was a few rungs higher up the ladder than them, and sharper, more intelligent. No other girl had ever had him in a corner explaining himself. He wouldn't have stood it from another girl. They were usually interested only in how good a time you could give them and how far they were prepared to let you go in return. They were easier to deal with: they took you for what you were and you didn't need your wits about you all the time as you did with this one. But they were none of them as attractive as she and not one of them had caused him to feel as he did now, dancing with her in his arms, quiet, at peace, the need for violence drained out of him so that he wished the music would never stop.

It was now after licensing hours and the hall had filled up with the latecomers from the closing pubs. The air, despite the open windows behind the long curtains, was thick and stifling and several times used. When the set ended they found themselves near the door. The girl pretended to fan herself with her open hand.

'I feel as if I'll never draw another breath. How much warmer can it get in here?'

'Let's go outside for a bit,' Vince suggested, 'an' get some air.'

He wondered what she was thinking as she looked at him.

'C'mon,' he said. 'I'll look after you. We can have a walk up the street an' back.'

'All right, then. This is getting a bit too much.'

They got pass-outs at the desk and stepped out into the street.

'Sure you'll be warm enough?' Vince asked, thinking of her thin blouse.

'Oh, yes: it's a mild night.'

She linked her arm through his as they walked up the quiet street and he glanced at her, feeling uplifted and happy. He knew nothing about her and began to ask her about herself. She lived in a street off Bradford Road, she told him, not far from where they had encountered her earlier that evening. She had an older sister who was married and a young brother still at school. Her father was an insurance superintendent and she was a typist in the main Cressley office of her father's company. She liked dancing, the cinema, records of Frank Sinatra, and swimming.

'Swimming?'

She told him how many lengths of the public baths she could swim and he was impressed.

'I should ha' thought with a figure like yours you'd be one o' them 'at never went in the water.'

She laughed. 'Swimming's good for the figure.'

'You're a good advert. I can't swim a stroke meself. I have to wear a lifebelt in the bath at home.'

'You'd soon learn with a bit of practice. It's like riding a bike – once you know how you can't imagine why everybody can't do it.'

'Oh, I can ride a bike. A motor bike an' all. I'm goinna get a motor bike. Next year mebbe.'

'A scooter?'

'Naw, a right bike. A six-fifty Norton, or summat like that. Summat with some power.'

'They're expensive. Have you been saving up?'

'I've got enough for a good deposit. It's a question of gettin' the old feller to sign the hire purchase papers, only he can't make his stupid mind up. He likes to act bloody awkward.'

'What do you do for a living?'

'I'm a motor mechanic. Why?'

'I just wondered.'

'You could tell I hadn't an office job by me hands, couldn't you?'

'What's wrong with your hands?'

'They show me trade. Grease an' stuff you can't get off.'

'They're a nice shape,' she said. 'I noticed. I always notice people's hands. There's nothing to be ashamed of in working with your hands. Do you like being a motor mechanic?'

He shrugged. 'It's okay. I like knackling with engines an' that. It's like every other job, though – you're just makin' brass for somebody else.'

'You're young. You can't do everything at once. Perhaps you'll have your own business one day.'

'Aw, I haven't got the brains for that sort o' thing. Messin' with books an' all that. An' anyway, where'd I get the capital?'

'Well you never know,' she said.

They made a circuit of the block and approached the Trocadero from the other side. As they walked along between the parked cars and the wall of the building Vince stopped and turned her round with his hands on her shoulders, feeling their smooth warmth through the blouse.

'Don't get panicky,' he said. 'I'm just goinna kiss you.'

'Who's panicky?' she said as his mouth came down on hers.

She was quiet at first, acquiescent but passive, her mouth cool and unresponsive under his. Then she parted her lips and put her arms about him. He felt a thrill of pure clear joy shoot through him as they broke away and stood close together in the shadow of the wall.

'I bet you never thought you'd end up like this when I saw you earlier on.'

She laughed. 'No, I didn't.'

'Neither did I, for that matter. I never expected to see you again . . . But I hoped I might.'

She was quiet.

'Will you let me see you again?'

'Do you really want to?'

'Yes, I do. I mean a proper date, where we arrange to meet each other an' there's just the two of us. Will you?'

'We'll see,' she said.

He dropped one hand from her shoulder to rest lightly on the swell of her breast and she lifted her own hand to remove it.

'Steady now.'

'Honest,' Vince said huskily. 'I'm not startin' anything. I'm not gettin' fresh. Honest. I wouldn't. I . . . I like you too much.'

The tenderness that overcame him as he held her was something new to him and appalling in the way it left him defenceless, drained of all violence, weak at the knees. She could do just what she liked with him, that was the way he felt about her. And under the joy it was frightening the way it made him think of things he had always scoffed at: things like steady courtship, marriage, a little home with someone to share it and be waiting for him at the end of the day.

'Oh, Christ!' he said as her mouth drew him again.

The beam of the flashlight picked them out as they stood embracing, mouth to mouth, body to body, against the wall. The shock of it was like cold water on them both. The girl hid her face but Vince turned his full into the beam of the torch, his eyes narrowing with fury as Jackson's voice said:

'I thought so. I thought that was what you were up to, you mucky little bugger. Bringing lasses out an' getting them up against the wall.'

Vince's heart pounded sickeningly. 'What the hell's up wi' you?' he said furiously. Hatred of Jackson scorched through him in a hot flood. 'Why can't you leave people alone? We're not doin' any harm.'

'I'm not having this sort o' work here,' Jackson said. 'You can either get back inside or clear off an' do your dirty work somewhere else. Come on, now, let's have you.'

He held the beam of the torch steadily on them as they walked to the corner of the building, the girl with her head bowed and Vince looking straight before him, biting his lip to restrain his wild rage.

Jackson walked away through the car park, leaving them in the light of the foyer. They went in, Vince showing the pass-outs.

The girl's face was scarlet with humiliation. Vince said, 'The swine; the lousy stinkin' swine.' He looked at her. 'God,' he said, 'I don't know what to say . . .'

She turned away from him, avoiding his eyes. 'It doesn't matter.'

'But look, I—'

'Leave me alone,' she said. 'Just leave me alone.'

He tried to take her arm. 'Look, Audrey . . .'

She shook herself free. 'My name's not Audrey.'

She hurried away from him into the cloakroom. He stood there for some moments until he became gradually aware of people watching him. His own cheeks burned as he went into the gents' cloakroom and shut himself in a cubicle. He was almost crying now with anger. He clenched his fists and beat them on the air, cursing Jackson silently through clenched teeth. He stayed there several minutes until he felt he could face returning to the hall. As he came into the foyer he caught a glimpse of a girl who looked like Iris hurrying out through the street door with a coat over her shoulders. He made a movement as if to follow her, then checked it and turned and went into the hall to find Sam and Finch and Bob. This was one thing Jackson wasn't going to get away with.

He found Sam first, alone, which was as he wanted it. He told him what had happened outside and how the girl had reacted.

'I don't know now if I'll ever see her again, Sam, or if she'll speak to me if I do. She's a chick with some class, Sam, see. It made her feel cheap being caught up against a wall like that. I know just how she feels, an' I'll allus remind her of it. Oh, that bloody lousy stinkin' pig Jackson.'

'He's a bloody maniac,' Sam said. 'Sex-mad. Where's the bird now?'

'I think she's hopped it. I thought I saw her goin' out just now.'

'An' where's Jacko?'

'He stopped outside playin' the bloody Peepin' Tom with his flashlamp.' Vince gripped Sam's arm. 'Listen, Sam, I'm goinna get that bugger for this. He's not gettin' away with it this time.'

'What you goinna do?'

'Wait for him on his way home an' do him. Are you with me? You'd like to have a go at him, wouldn't you?'

'Too bloody true I would,' Sam said. 'I haven't forgotten that night last winter when he picked on me an' threw me out of here. But it's no good just the two of us. Two of us can't manage him.'

'No, but we can if we have Finch an' Bob to back us up. We can bash the bugger till his own mother won't know him.'

Sam looked doubtful. 'Think they'll come?'

'Why not? They don't like Jacko any more than we do.'

'An' they don't like gettin' their earholes punched, either.'

'Oh, Christ Almighty, Sam, if the four of us can't manage him, I don't know who can. Where are they, anyway?'

'I think they're sittin' down the other end.'

'You get 'em. I'll go an' get a table in the coffee bar.'

A few minutes later the four of them were sitting round a corner table and Vince was telling the others what he had already told Sam. Bob appeared to find it amusing.

'What the hell you grinnin' at?' Vince demanded.

'Well, it's funny, in't it?' Bob said.

'I don't see owt bloody funny about it.'

'Well, there's a funny side to it, in't there?' Bob said. 'I mean, there's you standin' up again the wall with this tart an' along comes old Jacko an' shines his lamp on you.'

'You'd ha' thought it wa' funny if it'd been you, I suppose?' Vince said angrily. 'You'd ha' burst out laughin', I suppose?'

'No, I'd ha' been as mad as you,' Bob said. 'Only it wa'n't me, it wa' you.'

'An' that makes all the bloody difference, eh?'

'Well, I mean . . .' Bob subsided in the face of Vince's furious glare.

'I'll bet you could ha' killed him,' Finch said.

'If thoughts could kill he'd be lyin' out there stone dead this minute.'

'Let's get down to business,' Sam said. 'Time's gettin' on. They'll be slingin' everybody out of here afore long.'

'What's up?' Finch said.

'We're goinna do Jackson on the way home,' Vince told him; 'that's what's up.'

'Who's we?' Bob wanted to know.

'Me an' Sam; an' you an' Finch if you're game.'

Finch said nothing but gave a quick startled glance at the faces of Vince and Sam sitting opposite him.

'You an' Sam . . .' Bob said. 'Think you can manage him?'

'If we have to,' Vince said grimly. 'But it'll make it easier if you an' Finch join in.'

Still Finch remained silent.

'I dunno,' Bob said. 'He's a big bloke . . . fifteen or sixteen stone. An' he can use his fists. You've seen how he handles blokes he doesn't like.'

'Aye, tackling him'll be a bit different from kickin' a bloke in the ribs up a back alley,' Vince said.

Bob flushed. 'You know I'm not scared of a scrap. You know I allus hold me corner up.'

'I know you do, Bob.' Vince's voice was now conciliatory, but under it he wished furiously that he could upturn the table on them all in contempt and go and do what he had to do alone. 'You're a good lad in a scrap. That's why we want you with us. You don't like Jacko, do you? You'd like to have a hand in doin' him, wouldn't you?'

Bob looked at Sam, then at Vince.

'What's your plan?'

'Well, you know the skinny bastard won't pay for a taxi an' he allus walks home except when it's chuckin' it down with rain. I've been thinkin', if we go first an' wait on the edge of the common, just by the wood, we can jump him before he knows we're there.'

Sam nodded. 'That's a good idea. It's the best place, an' he'll never know who we are in the dark up there.'

'He won't even know how many of us there is,' said Vince. 'We can make mincemeat of the bastard an' drop down into town an' be home in bed by one.'

'Suppose he doesn't go that way tonight?'

'He allus does. An' if he doesn't we'll have to call it off till another time. But he'll be there; it's a nice night for a walk.'

'An' a good scrap,' Sam said, smiling.

Vince warmed to him. 'Good old Sam,' he said, putting his arm round the other's shoulders.

'Suppose he recognises us?' Bob said.

'Oh, Christ, suppose, suppose. He's got nothin' on us, has he? He can't prove anythin'. We can think of a story an' back one another up.'

Sam glanced at his watch, a large gold one with a gold strap that he had picked up for a pound late one night from a young National Service soldier who was too drunk to walk home and hadn't a shilling in his pocket towards taxi fare. 'We'd better be off if we're goin'. They'll be finishin' here any time now.'

Vince looked at Finch. 'What about you, Finch? You've said nowt so far.'

Finch hesitated before speaking. 'I reckon I'm game,' he said in a moment, 'if Bob is. Not if there's only three of us, though.'

'Good lad, Finch. You're a bloody trouper, you are. Now then, Bob, what about it?'

Bob played with a dirty cup which had not been cleared off the table before they sat down. He said nothing before Sam burst out impatiently:

'Oh, come on. What the hell's everybody ditherin' about? He's only one bloke against four of us. Let's get the bugger done. He's had it comin' to him for long enough.'

Bob decided, and pushed the cup away from him. 'Okay,' he said, 'I'm on.'

'That's the style,' Vince said exultantly. His eyes glittered in a face now flushed with excitement. He scraped back his chair. 'We'll half-kill the bastard. We'll give him summat to think about.'

The drums of the band were rolling for the National Anthem as they pushed a way through to the door. The dance was over. Jackson, they guessed, would be leaving in about fifteen minutes, which gave them time to approach the common by a roundabout route. Midnight struck from the clock tower of the Town Hall as they left the steep streets and took to an unsurfaced track along which they walked for a few minutes before leaving it for a narrow path across the rough grassland. They were quiet, speaking only occasionally and then in subdued voices, though the chance of their being seen or overheard here so late at night was remote. They were high up now above the town. Before them the path led on over the common to the Calderford Road and behind the darkness of the valley was pricked in a thousand places by the sparkle and glitter of street-lights. They left the path, swinging back in an arc towards the small wood on the town side, and now, for some time, no one spoke at all as they went on, lifting their feet high on the tussocky grassland.

Vince realised a few moments later that they had lost one of their number. 'Where the hell's Finch?' They stopped and turned, looking back the way they had come, as Finch came up after them at a run.

'Where the hell you been?'

'Stopped for a leak,' Finch said. 'I couldn't wait.'

'Thought you'd dropped down a rabbit hole,' Bob said, and Finch said 'Ha, ha!'

'For Christ's sake, keep with us,' Vince told him. 'We're nearly there.'

'I've never been up here in the dark afore,' Finch said. 'Glad I'm not by meself. It's a lovely spot for a murder.'

'Quiet,' Vince said. 'Don't talk 'less you have to.'

They reached the wood, which was no bigger than a large copse, and made a quick reconnaissance. They decided then to stick to Vince's original plan of lying in wait for Jackson just where the path entered the trees. Anyone using the path must surmount a small rise before dropping into the wood.

Vince said, 'I'll go up there an' keep a lookout. What time is it?'

Sam consulted the luminous face of his watch and said it was nearly a quarter past twelve.

'He shouldn't be long now.'

'If he comes at all,' Bob said.

'Course he'll come,' Vince said impatiently. 'He allus comes this way. It's his quickest way home when he's walkin'.'

He went forward to the summit of the hillock and as he stretched himself out on the cool grass the Town Hall clock struck the quarter hour. The moon was rising, lightening the sky. He hoped Jackson would not be too long or it might be light enough for him to recognise

them. And too long a wait might rob Finch and Bob of
their taste for the job. He wasn't worried about Sam.
He would stick. He was a good mate. Vince felt that he
could trust Sam as much as possible in a world where,
when it came right down to it, you could trust nobody;
where you depended on nobody but yourself and you
relied on people and used them just as much as you had
to, and no more. As he, if he admitted the truth, was
using the gang tonight for the purpose of wreaking his
personal revenge on Jackson. They none of them liked
Jackson, true; and each had his reasons for not being
sorry to see Jackson beaten up. But in none of them did
the pure hatred burn as fiercely as it did in Vince and
none of them would ever have made an attempt on
Jackson if he hadn't screwed them up to it tonight. It was a
performance he knew he could not repeat. It was tonight
or never. If Jackson chose this one night to change his
routine and go home another way, revenge was lost. And
if he didn't come in the next few minutes it might be too
late because already Vince could sense impatience in the
wood behind him as a voice murmured and he heard the
scrape of a match and saw its glow as some fool lit a
cigarette. He wanted to shout at them, but dared not.
He could only lie there waiting, hoping that Jackson
would come soon.

He looked out across the valley. The starless sky seemed
to be lifting and growing paler. He could make out the
shape of buildings, the looming bulk of mills and the
clock tower of the Town Hall. A car's headlights swooped
on Halifax Road. He heard the gear-change in the valley
bottom and the labour of the engine as it pulled away up
the hill. In the quiet that followed a man coughed in the
street beyond the fence and Vince's heart jumped. He

lay very still, his muscles tensed ready for flight to the wood. But there was no other sound, not even a footstep.

Finch came up beside him. 'Isn't there any sign of him?'

'Not yet. He'll come, though; there's still plenty of time.'

'Happen he's gone another way.'

'He allus comes this way.'

'He might have got himself a woman to take home.'

'He's wed. Got a couple o' kids, I believe.'

Finch grunted. He was crouching and Vince said, 'Keep yoursen down, can't you?'

Finch crouched a little lower. 'How much longer are we waitin'?'

'We'll give him a bit longer. He might have had a bit o' clearin' up to do, or summat.'

'Bob says he doesn't think he's comin' now.'

'Who the bloody hell cares what Bob thinks?' Vince hissed. 'Is that him smokin' that fag?'

'Yeh, he lit up a minute or two sin'.'

'Well get back to him an' tell him to bloody well put it out,' Vince said.

Finch disappeared and Vince lifted himself on his elbows. That Bob. He was more and more trouble every time they met. The time was coming fast when they would have to settle it once and for all. And one swift hard punch into Bob's face would do the trick. If Jackson didn't turn up it might be a way of relieving his feelings tonight, because Bob would be sure to have something to say about their having spent all this time on the common for nothing.

'Come on, Jackson,' he murmured. 'Come on, you big, stupid bastard, and get what's comin' to you.'

He began to think about the girl and he wondered if he would ever see her again. He remembered holding her and kissing her under the wall of the Trocadero and a lingering memory of tenderness touched his heart. Surely she wouldn't hold it against him for ever? Surely when she had calmed down and got over the humiliation she would realise that he, Vince, had not been able to help it? He had to see her again to find out. The Trocadero would be out after tonight because there would always be the fear that Jackson had known them. And Cressley was a big place. He could go for years and never run into her again. But perhaps she too would avoid the Trocadero now and go to the Gala Rooms, because she had said she liked dancing. She had also said she liked swimming, so he could always look for her at the baths. He would go to the baths every evening after work for a month if necessary, because he had to see her again, no matter what. He just had to.

His heart lifted then with sudden excitement as he became aware of somebody whistling down the hill. Jackson was coming, and whistling to keep himself company in the dark. He knew it was Jackson because he could recognise that whistle anywhere: light and musical and full of little runs and trills. He waited till Jackson's head and shoulders appeared at the stile, then slid down out of sight and ran back to join the others.

'He's comin'. Can you hear him whistlin'? We'll give the bastard summat to whistle about!'

They crouched on both sides of the path, hearing the scuff of a shoe-sole on a stone, then seeing Jackson's figure silhouetted against the lightening sky as he topped the rise.

'Remember,' Vince whispered. 'Don't talk.'

They closed with him as he came off the open common

and into the shadow of the trees. Vince had visualised the attack as being quick, concerted and silent. As it was, there was a moment's hesitation as they became visible to Jackson, as though no one knew who was to lead the assault.

Jackson stopped and stepped back. 'Now then, what's this?'

'You'll find out in a minute, Jackson!' Finch said, and Bob said quickly, but too late, 'Shurrup, fool!'

Jackson came for them, his fists at the ready. His first blow swung little Finch off his feet and sent him crashing helplessly into the bushes. Vince yelped as the toe of Jackson's shoe cracked against his shin. Then Jackson went down with Sam and Bob hanging on to him and Vince held back, rubbing his calf and waiting to see where he could help to best effect. He watched as the three bodies rolled about on the ground and heard the grunts and curses that came from them. Then the sound of someone crashing through the dry bracken diverted his attention and the next moment he saw Finch break clear of the wood and scurry up the path over the hillock. He opened his mouth to shout after Finch, then checked himself, muttering under his breath, 'The miserable little shit. The yellow little bleeder.'

Two of those struggling on the ground came to their feet, leaving the third bent almost double, holding his belly and moaning. Vince thought it was Sam. It wasn't going right. Jackson was too much even for the four of them. With Finch gone and Sam out of the fight it was time he looked to himself. But it was already too late. Jackson broke free of Bob's hug, felled him with a blow, and turned to Vince.

'Now you,' Jackson said. His voice was thick, as though

he was swallowing blood. He was breathing heavily too and he was unsteady on his feet. He had taken a lot of punishment from Sam and Bob but he was far from finished.

Vince cursed Finch again as he backed away. He knew that once Jackson closed with him he was done for. Before he hardly knew it the knife was open in his hand.

'Hold it, Jackson, or you'll get some o' this.' He flourished the weapon in an attempt at bravado and the blade glinted dully in the moonlight filtering down through the trees.

Jackson stopped for a second, then came on more slowly, his arms wide apart, his body poised ready to jump at the lunge of the knife. 'Don't be a bloody fool. Put that thing away before you hurt somebody.'

There was no reason left in Vince, only a sobbing rage and hatred for Jackson, who would beat him unmercifully if he once got in close enough. It had all gone wrong and it was Jackson's fault. Hatred seemed to swim in a hot wave before his eyes. He felt then the trunk of a tree behind him and knew he could retreat no farther without partly turning his back on Jackson. A trickle of warm liquid ran down the inside of his leg and he thought with stupid anger that he should have stopped when Finch had. His voice raised itself, shrill with fear and the knowledge that he was afraid.

'It'll be you 'at'll get hurt, Jackson. I'll carve the bloody tripes out of you, you dirty stinkin' bastard, if you come any nearer.'

Jackson came warily and steadily on, his eyes fixed on the blade of the knife.

'I've warned you. Keep back!'

There was a movement from behind Jackson. In the

same second he sprang, Bob jumped him from the rear and Vince drove forward and upward with the knife, the force of the blow taking his fist hard up against Jackson's belly. They all went down together in a heap.

Vince and Bob extricated themselves and got up together. They looked down at Jackson. There was blood on the fingers of Vince's right hand. He moved them and felt its sticky warmth. In a kind of daze he half lifted his hand to look.

'That's settled him,' Bob was saying. 'Now let's get out of here.' A second later he saw the knife. 'Christ, what you doin' with that?'

'I told him,' Vince said stupidly. 'I warned him he'd get it.' He touched Jackson's leg with the toe of his shoe. 'Jackson! Come on, now.'

'You've finished him,' Bob said. There was raw panic in his voice. 'Oh, Christ! Oh, Christ!'

Sam came up behind them, still rubbing his belly. 'God, me guts . . . What we hangin' about here for?'

'He's knifed him,' Bob said. 'The bloody fool's finished him.'

'Don't talk daft,' Vince said. 'He's okay. He's just reckonin'. We only roughed him up a bit, didn't we? That's all we said we'd do, in't it? Nobody said owt about killing the stupid bastard, did they?'

'Jesus,' Sam said. 'Oh, Christ Jesus. I'm not in this.'

'Me neither,' Bob said. 'I didn't do it. They can't touch me for it.'

He turned and blundered to the path, breaking into a run over the rise.

'Jackson!' Vince said. 'Give over reckonin', you lousy sod.' He pushed at Jackson with his foot. 'Jackson!'

He heard Sam say something from behind him but did

not take in the words. He dropped the knife and went down on his knees beside Jackson.

'Jackson. Come on, Jackson, wake up. I know you're actin'. You can't kid me. C'mon, you lousy dog, c'mon. Stop reckonin'!'

His hand came in contact with the mess of blood on the front of Jackson's shirt and he recoiled and stood up, staring in horror at the dark smear across his palm and fingers. It was as though this finally released in him a tremendous force of uncontrollable fury and hatred. He began to kick Jackson's body in a frenzy, assaulting it with savage blows of his feet and swearing in a torrent of words. And when, at last, he stopped, exhausted, his body suddenly sagging from the hips, his arms hanging limp at his sides, he raised his head and looked round. The moon rode from behind a ragged edge of cloud and the pale light fell on his upturned face. It was quiet. He was alone.